"You win the prize for the most infuriating woman I've ever met."

"Good," Millie said.

"As the mistress of the ruling sheikh of Khalifa, you'd have no competition—"

"Your *mistress*?" Millie repeated this as if she had something unpleasant on her tongue. "So, I'd have no competition for your attention. Is that right?"

"None," Khalid confirmed.

"Forget it, Your Majesty," she told him with an incredulous shake of her head. "Just tell me what I need to know, and we're done here."

He had an answer to that, and dipping his head, he enforced silence with a kiss. And not just any kiss, but one that melted her from the inside out. She only had to taste him, and she was lost. Khalid was everything that was missing from her life. His touch seared her senses. His kisses rocked her world. Being lost in his arms was the best prescription she knew for forgetting the past and living in the present. He offered oblivion, which was exactly what she craved. If she thought any more about events she couldn't change she'd go mad.

One Night With Consequences

When one night...leads to pregnancy!

When succumbing to a night of unbridled desire, it's impossible to think past the morning after!

But with the sheets barely settled, that little blue line appears on the pregnancy test, and it doesn't take long to realize that one night of white-hot passion has turned into a lifetime of consequences!

Only one question remains:

How do you tell a man you've just met that you're about to share more than just his bed?

Find out in:

The Pregnant Kavakos Bride by Sharon Kendrick

A Ring for the Greek's Baby by Melanie Milburne

Engaged for Her Enemy's Heir by Kate Hewitt

The Virgin's Shock Baby by Heidi Rice

The Italian's Christmas Secret by Sharon Kendrick

A Night of Royal Consequences by Susan Stephens

A Baby to Bind His Bride by Caitlin Crews

Claiming His Nine-Month Consequence by Jennie Lucas

Contracted for the Petrakis Heir by Annie West

Consequence of His Revenge by Dani Collins

Princess's Pregnancy Secret by Natalie Anderson

Look for more One Night With Consequences coming soon!

Susan Stephens

THE SHEIKH'S SHOCK CHILD

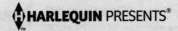
HARLEQUIN PRESENTS®

Recycling programs
for this product may
not exist in your area.

ISBN-13: 978-1-335-41946-0

The Sheikh's Shock Child

First North American publication 2018

Copyright © 2018 by Susan Stephens

Printed in U.S.A.

Susan Stephens was a professional singer before meeting her husband on the Mediterranean island of Malta. In true Harlequin style, they met on Monday, became engaged on Friday and married three months later. Susan enjoys entertaining, travel and going to the theater. To relax she reads, cooks and plays the piano, and when she's had enough of relaxing she throws herself off mountains on skis or gallops through the countryside, singing loudly.

Books by Susan Stephens

Harlequin Presents

The Sicilian's Defiant Virgin
In the Sheikh's Service
Italian Boss, Proud Miss Prim

One Night With Consequences

A Night of Royal Consequences
Bound to the Tuscan Billionaire

Secret Heirs of Billionaires

The Secret Kept from the Greek

Wedlocked!

A Diamond for Del Rio's Housekeeper

Hot Brazilian Nights!

In the Brazilian's Debt
At the Brazilian's Command
Brazilian's Nine Months' Notice
Back in the Brazilian's Bed

Visit the Author Profile page
at Harlequin.com for more titles.

For Megan, for excellent editing and steely nerve.
Thank you.

CHAPTER ONE

SAPPHIRES DRIFTED IN a shimmering stream from the Sheikh's fingers. Backlit by candlelight, the precious gems blazed with blue fire, dazzling fifteen-year-old Millie Dillinger. Seeing her mother cuddled up to the Sheikh had the opposite effect. Toad-like and repellent, he was hardly the dashing hero Millie had imagined when her mother had said they were both to be guests at a most important royal engagement.

Millie had just stepped on board the Sheikh's superyacht after being brought straight from school in a limousine with diplomatic plates, and found this a very different and frightening world. Sumptuous yes. Everywhere she looked there were more obvious signs of money than she'd seen in her entire life, but, like the Sheikh, the interior of his vast, creaking superyacht was sinister, rather than enticing. She kept glancing over her shoulder to check for escape routes, knowing it wouldn't be easy to go anywhere with heavily armed guards, dressed in black tunics and baggy trousers, standing on either side of her, with yet more posted around the room.

Much in Millie's life was uncertain, but this was frightening. Her mother was unpredictable, and it was always up to Millie to try and keep things on an even keel. That meant getting them out of here, if she could. This big room was known as the grand salon, but when she'd seen pictures in magazines of similar vessels, they were light and elegant, luxurious spaces, not dark and stale like this. Heavy drapes had been closed to shut out the light, and it smelled bad. Like an old wardrobe, Millie thought, wrinkling her nose.

The Sheikh and his guests were staring at her, making her feel she was part of a show, and it was not a performance she wanted to take part in. Seeing her mother in the arms of an old man was bad enough. He might be royalty, and he might be seated in the place of honour on a bank of silken cushions beneath a golden canopy, but he was repulsive. This had to be their host, His Magnificence Sheikh Saif al Busra bin Khalifa. Millie's mother, Roxy Dillinger, had been hired to sing at his party, and had asked Millie to join her. Why? Millie wondered.

'Hello, little girl.' The Sheikh spoke in a wheedling tone that made Millie shudder. 'You are most welcome here,' he said, beckoning her closer.

She refused to move as her mother prompted in a slurred stage whisper, 'Her name is Millie.'

As if names were unimportant to him, the Sheikh beckoned again, and more impatiently this time. Millie stared at her mother, willing her to make her excuses so that they could leave. Her mother refused to take the hint. She was still so beautiful, but sad for much of the time, as if she knew her days in the sun were over. Millie wanted to protect her, and quivered with indignation when some of the guests began to snigger behind their hands. Sometimes it felt as if she were the grown up and her mother the child.

'See, Millie,' her mother exclaimed as she raised and slopped a glass of champagne down an evening dress that had seen better days. 'This is the type of life you can have if you follow me onto the stage.'

Millie shrank at the thought. Her dream was to be a marine engineer. This was more like Walpurgis Night than a theatrical performance, with every witch and warlock gathered to carouse and feast at the feet of the devil. Candlelight flickered eerily over the faces of the guests, and an air of expectation gripped them. What were they waiting for? Millie wondered. She didn't belong here, and neither did her mother, and if her mother started to sing it would be worse. A care-less approach to her health had ruined Roxy Dillinger's renowned singing voice. She had squeezed herself into a shoddy and revealing floor-length gown, but Millie knew that the best she would be able to manage was a few cigarette-scarred songs for people who didn't care that Roxy had once been known as the Nightin-gale of London.

Millie cared. She cared deeply and passionately for her mother, and her protective instinct rose like a lion for its cub. Ignoring the impatience of the Sheikh, she held out her hands. 'It's time to go home. Please, Mum—'

'Roxy,' her mother hissed, shooting a warning glance at Millie. 'My name is Roxy.'

'Please… Roxy,' Millie amended reluctantly. Whatever it took, she would get them out of here somehow.

'Don't be stupid,' her mother snapped, staring round at her less than admiring public. 'I haven't sung yet. Tell you what,' she said in a change of tone. 'Why don't you sing for us, Millie? She has a lovely voice,' she added to the Sheikh. 'Not as strong and pure as mine, of course,' she added, snuggling up to him.

The way the Sheikh was looking at Millie made her skin crawl, but she refused to back down. 'If you come home with me now, I'll buy cakes on the way,' she coaxed her mother.

Unpleasant laughter greeted this remark. A gesture from the Sheikh silenced his guests. 'I have world-renowned pastry chefs on board, little girl. You and your mother can eat your fill—once you've sung for your supper.'

Millie suspected the Sheikh had something else in mind other than singing. With her plaits, spectacles and serious demeanour, she would certainly be a novelty for his sophisticated guests, who had started to chant her name. Far from this being encouragement, as her mother seemed to think, Millie knew it was mockery of the cruellest kind. Her neck burned with embarrassment as she begged, 'Please, Mum. You don't need the Sheikh's money. I'll take an extra shift at the laundry—'

Screeches of laughter drowned out her voice. Desperate now, she glanced longingly in the direction of the marina, where life would be carrying on as normal. If this was how the super-rich lived, Millie wanted no

part of it. Tonight had cemented her decision to forge
a life she could control.

'Sing for us, Millie,' Roxy slurred. 'You can be my
support act.'

Millie loved singing, and had joined the school
choir, but her real passion was discovering how things
worked. Once she'd passed her school exams, she was
determined to put in as many hours as it took, working at the laundry to fund more education.

The crowd continued to chant, *'Millie... Millie...
Millie...'* Her mother's eye make-up was smudged,
and she looked so tired. 'Please, Mum...'

'You'll stay here,' the toad on the dais rapped. At his
signal, the guards closed around Millie, cutting off all
avenues of escape. 'Come closer, little girl,' he drawled
in a sugary voice that frightened her. 'Dip your hands
into my bowl of sapphires. They will inspire you, as
they have inspired your mother.'

Millie flinched away as someone shrieked an ugly
laugh.

'Touch my sapphires,' the Sheikh continued in the
same hypnotic tone. 'Feel their cool magnificence—'

'Step back!'

The icy command was delivered like a shot and
shocked everyone rigid. Millie turned to see a co-
lossus in travel clothes striding into their midst. The
guards snapped to attention as he passed, and even the
Sheikh's spoiled mouth remained petulantly closed.

What a devastating man, Millie thought. Much
younger than the Sheikh, he was infinitely more attractive, and Millie's ideal when it came to a romantic

hero. While the Sheikh overflowed his cushions, this man was lean and fit, like a soldier or a bodyguard.

'Why, *brother*, you're such a prude.'

When the Sheikh drawled this, she gasped. His *brother*? *This* was the toad's brother? There was so little resemblance between the two men it didn't seem possible. While the Sheikh sent shivers of disgust shooting down her spine, his brother inspired a very different response.

She cringed to see the Sheikh wrap his arms a little closer around her mother, as if claiming his property in the face of a challenge. 'Have you never played Bridge the Generation Gap before?' he asked, glancing between the newcomer, Millie, and her mother.

'You disgust me,' the newcomer rapped. 'She's just a child,' he observed as he flashed an appraising glance at Millie.

That brief look seared her to the depth of her soul. She would never forget it. There was anger in his eyes, but also concern, and it made her feel safe for the first time since she'd boarded the yacht.

'I can't believe you'd sink so low as to include a young girl in your debauchery,' he said scathingly.

'Can't you?' The Sheikh gave a careless shrug. 'She's a pretty young thing. Why don't you take a turn when I'm finished with her?'

'You and I are very different, brother.'

'Evidently,' the Sheikh conceded. 'But it's no business of yours how I spend my free time.'

'When you bring our country into disrepute, it is my business.'

The Sheikh's striking-looking brother had everyone's interest, Millie noticed, and no wonder, with his skin the colour of polished bronze, and that thick, jet-black wavy hair. His body was as powerful as a gladiator's, his eyes as fierce and unforgiving as a hawk's, while harsh cheekbones and sweeping inky brows added to the exotic picture of a man who commanded the room.

'You sicken me,' he rapped with disgust. 'I return from fighting alongside our forces, to find you indulging yourself in the most depraved manner imaginable. You won't be satisfied until you've brought our country to its knees.'

'I'll bring something to its knees,' the Sheikh agreed with a lascivious glance at Millie.

Millie gasped as the younger man swept a protective arm around her shoulder. 'You won't touch her,' he warned.

The Sheikh's response was a lazy wave of his hand. 'You take things too seriously, Khalid. You always did.'

Khalid.

Learning her guardian's name, Millie felt a rush of emotion. He remained standing between her and the Sheikh, to protect her from his brother's crude remarks and lewd glances. If only he could rescue her mother too.

'Don't bring your bleeding heart here,' the Sheikh dismissed with a scornful look. 'It's not appreciated.'

'A bleeding heart because I care for our people?' the Prince challenged, stepping away from Millie. 'Where were you when our country needed you, Saif?' he demanded. 'You left our borders unprotected and our people in danger. You should be ashamed of yourself,' he finished with icy disdain.

'It is you who should be ashamed for ruining the evening for my guests,' the Sheikh remarked, unconcerned. 'And it is you who should apologise,' he insisted.

Shaking his head, Prince Khalid assured his brother that he would do no such thing. 'Come,' he added sharply to Millie. 'You're leaving right now. And if you had any sense,' he added to Millie's mother, 'you'd leave too.'

Roxy's response was to turn her sulky face into the Sheikh's shoulder.

'Is this what *you* want?' the Sheikh asked Millie.

'Yes,' Millie almost shouted, 'but I'm not leaving without my mother. Please—' It was useless. Her mother didn't move.

'At least take some sapphires with you,' the Sheikh suggested in a mocking tone.

'Don't touch them!' his brother rapped.

'As if I would!' This time she did shout, and it was so unlike her to lose her temper, but if he thought for one moment she could be bribed with sapphires!

Prince Khalid smiled faintly as he looked at her, and there was almost respect in his eyes, Millie thought, as if he knew she found this situation as deplorable as he did.

'You're a disgrace to the Khalifa name,' her rescuer thundered, turning his attention to Sheikh Saif. 'If you weren't the ruler of Khalifa—'

'What would you do?' the Sheikh queried in an

oily tone. 'I stand between you and the throne. Is that what's really troubling you, brother?' Opening his arms wide, the Sheikh drew in his avid audience. 'My poor brother can never get over the fact that he can't have things all his own, dull way. How boring life would be with you in charge of the country, Khalid.'

This was greeted by murmurs of agreement from his guests. Millie risked a glance to see how the Prince had taken this latest insult. Apart from a muscle flicking in his jaw, he remained unmoved. 'I'm taking the girl,' he said, 'and I want the mother gone by the time I return. Her daughter should not be left alone at night with so many unpleasant characters roaming King's Dock.'

A gasp of affront greeted this remark. The Sheikh remained unconcerned. 'But she won't be on her own, will you, my dear? She'll have you,' he added with a sneer for Prince Khalid.

By this time, Millie was consumed with fear for her mother. 'I can't leave her,' she told the Prince when he tried to usher her away.

Gripping her arm firmly, he warned, 'Don't get any ideas. You're leaving now.'

'Not without my mother,' Millie said stubbornly.

'Get her out of here!' her mother yelled with an angry gesture in Millie's direction.

Having finally dislodged herself from the Sheikh's embrace, her mother was standing with her fists tightly clenched. 'You're nothing but a little killjoy,' she railed at Millie. 'You always spoil my fun!'

Gasping with hurt, Millie was barely aware that the

door of the grand salon had slammed behind her, making her last memory of that night her mother's voice screaming at her to go.

'What's your name?' he asked the pale, tense child as he escorted her off the *Sapphire*. He needed something to distract her from the ordeal, and wanted to keep her talking. She seemed so unnaturally quiet.

There was a silence and then, to his relief, she said in a strained whisper, 'Millicent.'

'Millicent?' he repeated. 'I like your name.' It suited the girl with her serious demeanour, heavy glasses and neatly braided hair.

'People call me Millie,' she added shyly as they left the shadows behind and exited the vessel into clean ocean air.

The child was as refreshing as the ocean, he thought, and he was determined to do what he could to protect her from harm. 'What do you like to be called?' he asked when she turned back to stare up at the shaded windows behind which they both knew her mother would continue to party.

'Me?' She frowned and then refocused on his face. 'I like to be called Millie.'

'Millie,' he repeated.

'Will you do something for me?' she asked, surprising him with her quick recovery.

'If I can,' he agreed.

They had reached the head of the gangplank, where she drew to a halt. 'Will you tell my mother to leave?' she begged earnestly. 'She might listen to you. Will you find her a cab and send her home? I've got some money. I can pay you—'

'You've got your bus fare home?' he guessed. She was young, but she was sensible. She had to be, he thought.

'Yes,' she confirmed. Her forehead pleated with surprise, as if common sense were second nature to the daughter, if not the mother. 'Of course I do. Well? Will you?' she pressed.

'I'll see what I can do,' he agreed.

'Please,' she pressed. 'Promise me you'll try.'

Something about her steady gaze compelled him to answer in the affirmative. 'I promise. Now go home and do your school work.'

He followed her gaze with interest as something else occurred to her. She was staring at his brother's chauffeur, who was standing stiffly to attention at the side of the royal limousine. He saluted as Khalid approached.

'He's been standing here for ages,' Millie whispered discreetly. 'Could you bring him a glass of water before he takes me home?'

'Me?' he exclaimed.

'Why not you?' she demanded. 'There's nothing wrong with your legs, is there?'

Her cheeky comment took him by surprise. She had spirit, and to spare.

'He brought me here,' she explained, 'so I know he must be tired.'

Completely unaware of status or rank, she was a novelty, and a welcome reminder that their respective positions in life had been decided by an accident of birth. Her cheeks blushed red as he pointed out the iced water dispensers, both in the front and the back of the vehicle. 'He's fine,' he explained in the same confiding tone. 'Give him your address and he'll see you home safely.'

'And my mother?' she said, staring back at the ship.

'I'll do what I can.' He ground his jaw with disgust at the prospect of returning on board. 'Never put yourself in such danger again,' he added in his sternest tone.

She didn't flinch as she retorted fiercely, 'I never will.'

He watched the vehicle pull away with its lonely figure seated upright in the back. With her school satchel at her side, and her hands folded neatly on her lap, Millie stared straight ahead. It was impossible to imagine a greater contrast to her mother, and his last thought before turning to the ship was that Millie was a good girl who deserved better than this.

CHAPTER TWO

Eight years later...

'OKAY, IT'S WORKING AGAIN.' Satisfied with her handiwork, Millie stepped away from the boiler she'd just repaired.

'You're a gem,' Miss Francine, the octogenarian who had worked at the laundry since she was a girl, and who now owned the business, beamed at Millie as she enveloped her favourite worker in a hug. 'I don't know anyone else who has the patience to coax these old machines back to life. What would I do without you?'

'We'd go down to the stream and beat the yachties' sheets clean with stones,' a girl called Lucy suggested dryly.

With a grin for her friend, Millie plucked a pencil from her bundled-up hair to make notes on how to start up the ancient boiler should it fail when she had returned to her apprenticeship as a marine engineer.

'You'd better not beat the Sheikh of Khalifa's *golden* sheets clean,' Lucy observed, matching Millie's grin.

'He might keel-haul you, or... *What?*' she demanded when both Millie and Miss Francine froze in horror.

'Nothing,' Millie said quietly, forcing her face to relax as she flashed a warning look at Miss Francine to say nothing. 'I didn't know the Sheikh's yacht had berthed, that's all.'

Lucy flung her arms wide like a proud fisherman demonstrating the improbable size of his latest catch. 'It's enormous! You couldn't miss it, if you hadn't had your head stuck in the boiler cupboard.'

Then, thank goodness she had, Millie thought.

'When did those sheets come in?' Miss Francine asked, obviously trying to distract from a topic she knew Millie would not want to discuss.

Lucy held out the yards of gold fabric overflowing her arms. 'The housekeeper from the *Sapphire* brought them, saying they needed special handling.'

'Ripping up?' Millie suggested beneath her breath. The golden sheets reminded her of one particular night and all its heartwrenching associations.

Miss Francine stepped in to her rescue again. 'If a yacht the size of the *Sapphire* has berthed, we must get back to work. We'll have laundry coming out of our ears,' she enthused, with an anxious look at Millie. 'And it might be the pressing machine that goes next.'

'Well, I'm here if it does break down,' Millie soothed, appreciating the change of subject.

'Are you sure you're all right?' Miss Francine asked discreetly as soon as everyone else was distracted by work.

'I'm fine,' Millie confirmed, 'and happy to take responsibility for those sheets. I'll supervise their care every step of the way,' she assured her elderly friend grimly, 'and I'll take them back on board to make sure they're fitted properly.'

'There's no need for that,' Miss Francine said, flashing Millie a concerned look. 'I'll take them.'

'I want to,' Millie insisted. 'It's a matter of pride.' She had to prove to herself that she could do this, and after eight years of hunting for clues into her mother's death, this was the best lead she'd had.

'Well, if you're happy to do it, I won't argue with you,' Miss Francine confirmed. 'We'll have more than enough work to go round.'

Something about the way her elderly friend had capitulated so quickly rang alarm bells in Millie's head. Which she dismissed as overreaction. Discovering the *Sapphire* was back was a shock.

'What do you think of the golden sheets?' Lucy asked later as they worked side by side.

'Magnificent, I suppose,' Millie admitted, 'but too gaudy for my taste.' Though typical of the *Sapphire*, she thought, grinding her jaw as pictures of gemstones falling from a hand that might have pushed her mother to her death swam into her mind.

'Too gaudy for mine too,' Lucy agreed.

'Try not to think about it,' Miss Francine whispered as she drew Millie to one side. 'Take a few deep breaths,' she advised.

If only breathing steadily could be enough to shut out the past. *'I gave birth at sixteen, you know,'* her mother had told the Sheikh.

Why must Millie always remember the bad things? *But that wasn't the worst, was it?*

Ignoring her mother's comment with a derisive eye-roll, the Sheikh had remarked, 'Of course you did,' as he selected a ripe fig with his fat, bejewelled fingers.

'I was never meant to have a child,' her mother had added with a scowl for Millie.

Millie still felt the pain of that comment and remembered how her mother had snuggled even deeper into the Sheikh's reptilian embrace as she'd said it, shutting out Millie completely—

'Millie?'

'Yes?' She forced a bright note into her voice as Miss Francine came around to double-check she was okay. 'So, he's back,' Millie remarked, trying to sound upbeat.

Her old friend wasn't convinced by her act. 'It seems so,' Miss Francine agreed briskly as she helped Millie to tuck the fabulous sheets into a fine cotton sack they used for the most delicate fabrics before washing them.

'He's been gone a long time,' Millie added in a lame attempt to keep the conversation alive. 'I guess Sheikh Saif had to stay out of the country after the accident.'

'Millie,' Miss Francine interrupted in a concerned tone.

Millie had never seen her elderly friend looking so worried. 'What is it? What's wrong?' she asked.

'I should have told you right away,' Miss Francine explained with a regretful shake of her head. 'It isn't Sheikh Saif on board the *Sapphire*. He died some years ago—of overeating, the press said,' she added with a grimace for Millie, who was too shocked to speak. 'You were away on that oil rig as part of your work experience when he died.'

'Who then?' Millie managed to force out. 'Who's on the *Sapphire*?'

'His brother, Sheikh Khalid,' Miss Francine revealed in a businesslike manner Millie had no doubt was gauged to cause her the least distress.

Nothing helped. Millie felt as if all the air had been sucked out of her lungs as Miss Francine continued, 'Sheikh Saif's death only made a few column inches in the press, and you were so upbeat when you came home that I couldn't bear to dampen your enthusiasm by bringing up the past.'

'Thank you,' Millie said numbly.

'You don't have to thank me for anything,' Miss Francine insisted as she rested a reassuring hand on Millie's shoulder.

There was nothing more to say, and they both fell silent. Millie had been a Saturday girl at the laundry at the time of her mother's tragic death, Miss Francine had stepped in right away, offering her a place to live. Home had been a room above the laundry ever since.

'Of course, no one mentioned Sheikh Saif's death to me,' Millie mused dazedly, 'because...' She shrugged. 'Why would they?'

Was she imagining it, or was Miss Francine finding it hard to meet her eyes?

'I owe you everything,' she said, giving her elderly friend an impulsive hug.

When Miss Francine left her side, Millie put her work on autopilot, so she could think back to what she remembered about Prince Khalid. Which was quite a lot. Never had anyone made such a strong impression on her. Most of it good. All of it awe-inspiring. And confusing. She'd thought him one thing, which was hero material, but he'd turned out to be something very different. And she must think of him as *Sheikh* Khalid now, Millie amended as images of blazing masculinity came flooding back. The sternest of men was now an omnipotent ruler. She could only imagine the changes in him. A few minutes in his company had been enough to brand his image on her soul. She could still see him striding up the *Sapphire*'s gangplank like an avenging angel to rescue her mother. But he hadn't rescued her mother. He'd let her down. And at some point during that terrible night, Millie's mother had either fallen from the *Sapphire*, or she'd been pushed.

Bracing herself, she stared out of the window. It was impossible to miss the *Sapphire* at rest in its berth. The superyacht was as big as a commercial cruise liner, and easily the biggest ship in the harbour. It was like a call to destiny that she couldn't avoid. She tried not to show how tense she was when Miss Francine came back. 'It's had a complete refit,' her elderly friend explained. 'When Sheikh Khalid inherited the throne of Khalifa from his brother, he insisted that the ship must be gutted and refitted. Gossip on the marina says that everything on board is cutting edge.' There was a long pause, and then she added carefully, 'Nothing ever remains the same, Millie.'

'I'm sure you're right,' Millie agreed. She knew Miss Francine was just trying to help. 'And *I'm* all right,' she added briskly, with a reassuring smile for her friend. 'However fabulous the *Sapphire* looks, it has moving parts that need to be fixed.'

Miss Francine laughed as Millie hoped she would. 'Taking your tool kit on board?' she suggested.

Millie narrowed her eyes. 'You can bet I'll be fully prepared by the time I board.'

'I'm sure you will be,' Miss Francine agreed quietly.

'My life is here with you,' Millie said. 'And it's very different from the life I had at fifteen. You've given me a happy home where I'm safe, and a launch pad so I can work towards a successful career. I'll never be able to thank you enough for that.'

'I don't want your thanks,' Miss Francine assured her. 'I couldn't love you more if you were my daughter.'

As they hugged, Millie reflected that she certainly didn't owe the Sheikh of Khalifa anything, other than contempt for letting her down. He was on board the *Sapphire* the night of her mother's death, and when the authorities had come calling, he'd made sure to keep his brother out of the courts.

'I'll take the sheets on board, and be back before you know it,' she said with confidence. She was grimly determined to do just that, if only to prove to herself that the past couldn't hurt her.

Miss Francine exclaimed with relief, 'Bravo!'

Dressed in formal, flowing black silk robes trimmed with gold, Khalid was looking forward to reclaiming the informality he enjoyed on board the *Sapphire*, but before he could relax he had business to attend to. He had just received a deputation from the local council asking for his support with its youth plan, which accounted for his dress code of regal opulence. This world tour had lasted long enough, he concluded as he appended a final signature to the document that would fund his latest project. Staring out through the rain-lashed windows of his study, he reflected on the significance of King's Dock. His educational trust had been born here, because of an incident that had changed his life. He had never thought to return, but neither would he neglect an opportunity to help young people gain a foothold in life. He had been asked for help, so he was here, and now he was here he couldn't leave without having reassured himself about certain issues.

Closing his eyes, he eased his neck. He longed for the cleansing heat of the desert and the cooling waters of the oasis, but the truth of that terrible night wouldn't go away. Pushing back from his desk, he stood up, and was glad of a muted tap on the door to distract him.

'Come...'

His housekeeper entered and stood politely just inside the entrance. 'The Gilded Stateroom is almost ready for your inspection, Your Majesty.'

'Thank you. Please let me know when the final touches have been made, and I'll inform you if I require anything else.'

'Of course, Your Majesty.' With a curtsey his housekeeper left the room.

He didn't check every guest room, but this was

for a particular guest, his old friend Tadj. Otherwise known as His Radiance, the Emir of Qalala, Tadj and he had been friends since school and university, and had joined Special Forces together. Khalifa and Qalala were trading partners, with valuable sapphire mines adjacent to each other in the mountains of Khublastan. The boundaries of several countries converged in this same region, which had led to their rulers becoming known collectively as the Sapphire Sheikhs. He was looking forward to Tadj's arrival. Things were stable again in Khalifa after Saif's tumultuous reign, and Khalid had not taken a break for some years. Having built a strong team around him, he could afford to do so now. This trip was an opportunity to build relationships between nations, and also to give him the chance to view the royal marriage mart to see if any of the available princesses would do. Tadj might advise on that—then again not, he thought dryly. Tadj was the devil incarnate where women were concerned.

Not wishing to dwell on thoughts of marriage, Khalid returned in his mind to Khalifa, that most beautiful of countries. Prosperity in the last few years had led to modern cities rising like mirages out of the ocean of sand, and though the desert might seem hostile to a casual visitor, it was teeming with life, especially around the oases where the animals he loved, the ibex and desert oryx, thrived beneath his protection. A crystalline ocean yielded more than enough food for his people, while a dramatic snow-capped mountain range held the precious seams of sapphires that gave them security, wealth, education, and medical care. To him there was nowhere to compare with Khalifa, and his spirits soared as he thought about the country he loved.

The stateroom for Tadj!

As he turned to leave his study something drew his glance to the window where, far below him on the rain-swept dock, a mini-drama was playing out. A small figure cloaked head to foot in sensible oilskins was attempting to gain entry onto the private walkway leading to the *Sapphire*. A sentry stood in her way. He could tell it was a woman from her height and tiny hands, with which she was gesturing vigorously as if to impress upon the guard that her mission was urgent and she must be allowed on board. She had a large, wheeled container at her side, and it was this that his security personnel, quite rightly, was intent on searching.

'No,' she told them with a decisive shake of her head, staring to the sky, as if to point out the obvious: that the rain would ruin her goods. A quick-thinking guard stepped forward with a sniffer dog. Once the dog had made a comprehensive inspection, she was allowed to pass.

Satisfied that she would be accompanied every inch of the way, he pulled back from the window. His guests would be arriving soon for a glamorous evening, so it came as no surprise to him to discover that deliveries were being made.

An officer greeted him as he left the study. 'A message from the mine, Your Majesty.'

'Oh?' Concern struck him as it always did where work underground was concerned. This would mean a delay to his inspection of Tadj's quarters, but the depths of the earth, like the deeps of the ocean, were unpredictable territory and inherently dangerous, and the safety of his staff was paramount.

'Good news, Majesty.'

He relaxed. 'Tell me...'

The officer could hardly contain his excitement. 'The new seam of sapphires is almost ten times larger than first thought, Your Majesty.'

'Good news, indeed!'

Returning to his study, he placed a call to congratulate his team. As he waited for the line to connect, his thoughts returned to the young woman on the dock. She'd be on board by now, with his security guard in attendance. No visitor would ever wander the *Sapphire* unattended again. After the tragedy under his brother's rule, Khalid had vowed that he would never take a chance with another person's life.

'Ah, Jusef,' he exclaimed as the line connected. He enjoyed an upbeat exchange with the manager of his mine, ending with the promise, 'I'll be home soon to celebrate with you.'

It was a good enough reason to postpone his search for a bride, and he left his study in the best of moods. A final glance through the window reminded him of the girl, and he smiled to think of her standing up to his guards, *and* getting her own way. That was no mean feat. His guards were ferocious.

There was just time to check the arrangements being made for Tadj, before taking a shower and preparing for the evening ahead. It would be a very different party from those his late brother had held on board the *Sapphire*, in that the people present would be interesting and stimulating company and there would be no wild excesses of any kind. Saif had been furious to have his pleasure curtailed, and had ordered Khalid off the *Sapphire*. Echoing the words of the girl's mother, he'd accused Khalid of being a killjoy.

Better that than a killer, Khalid had always thought.

CHAPTER THREE

RETURNING TO THE *Sapphire* wasn't as easy as Millie had imagined. Her heart had started thundering out of control the moment she'd set foot on deck. However many times she told herself that this was a rite of passage, and she must get through it, her body's reaction was out of her control.

I'm not a teenager, finding my way and feeling awkward, but a successful woman, confident in my own skin.

She had silently chanted this mantra from the moment she'd entered the locked dock. The past couldn't hurt her, if she didn't allow it to. The emotional scars from that night hadn't weakened her, they'd made her strong. Unfortunately, none of these self-administered reassurances helped to soothe her as she stepped onto the recently swabbed teak and all the memories came flooding back. Her throat dried when the guard beckoned her towards the impressive double doors leading into the interior of the vessel.

Taking a deep breath, she braced herself and walked in.

The first thing she noticed was the lack of a sickly-sweet smell. She hadn't known what it was eight years ago, but now her best guess was cannabis. The air inside the vessel today was as clean and as fresh as the air outside. And there wasn't a speck of dust to be seen, let alone a carelessly stubbed out cigarette, or an empty bottle left to roll aimlessly about. There was certainly no jarring music, or cruel laughter, just the low, almost indiscernible hum of a well-maintained engine of the type Millie loved—

She jerked alert as the guard coughed to attract her attention. 'Sorry to keep you,' she said. 'I was just getting my bearings.'

A steward was on hand to take charge of her oilskins and the wheeled trolley. Watching her oilskins disappear around a corner definitely gave her second thoughts. She wanted to call him back and return to the safety of the laundry.

Don't be so ridiculous!

What about her determination that the past couldn't hurt her? And the note she intended to leave for Sheikh Khalid, asking if he could make time to see her.

Where was he? she wondered. Somewhere on board? Somewhere close?

A ripple of awareness tracked down her spine. Her overactive imagination getting busy again, she concluded as the steward returned to her side. He suggested, and tactfully, she thought in view of the state of her trolley, that it might be an idea to unpack the laundry here.

'Yes, of course,' she said. 'I'm sorry. I didn't realise the wheels were quite so muddy.' Or that they would leave such obvious tracks on the pristine floor. Not wanting to cause extra work for the crew, she was glad of the blue plastic overshoes the steward handed her.

She was sorry about everything, Millie thought, which was hardly the mind-set required to make the most of this opportunity. The steward might pass on a note to someone in authority who had contact with the Sheikh. And though Sheikh Khalid almost certainly wouldn't agree to see her, she had to try.

'I'll help you unpack,' the friendly steward offered.

The Sheikh's staff seemed nice. She took some comfort from that. There were no stony faces—apart from his guards—and the atmosphere was different; very different, Millie thought as she introduced herself.

'Joel,' the steward replied with a friendly smile.

After a brief handshake they got to work, and the familiar actions of lifting the laundry from its nest reassured her. She knew what she was doing, and working side by side with Joel boosted her confidence. His uniform was very smart, and not at all intimidating, as she remembered the black-clad servants at that *other* party. Crisp and white, it was quite a contrast to her comfortable work clothes of jeans, a long-sleeved top and sneakers.

If it came to running for it, she was ready, Millie concluded dryly as she straightened up to announce she was ready to make up the bed. The guard would escort them, he said. Things had certainly changed since the free-for-all days of Sheikh Saif, she thought as they set off at a brisk walk with Millie like a sandwich filling between the two men.

Passing through another set of double doors, they

entered a world of unimaginable luxury and calm.
Or massive wealth and relentless control, depending
on how you looked at it. Either she found some humour in this situation, or she'd lose her nerve and run.
She couldn't believe the last time she'd been here her
mother was alive. It seemed so long ago. And now
her senses were heightened to an unparalleled degree.
She felt like a sponge, obliged to soak up everything,
whether she wanted to or not. Though she had to admit
that the vibrant works of art, tastefully displayed on
neutral walls, were beautiful, as were the priceless
artefacts housed in glass cases. She would have loved
the chance to take a longer look at them. Glimpses into
staterooms as they passed revealed one luxurious setting after another, but the walk was so long, she began
to wonder if they would ever arrive at their destination.
The *Sapphire* was bigger than she remembered, but
then she had only seen the grand salon eight years ago.

I could get lost here and never be heard of again.
Like my mother.

That imagination of hers was working overtime
again. She was here to work, and when that was done,
she was out of here!

Millie Dillinger, Khalid mused as he strode through
the immaculately maintained vessel in the direction of
the guest quarters. The girl's name would be branded
on his mind for ever. How could he ever forget the dramatic events surrounding their first encounter? He'd
been in a furious mood that night, too angry by what
he'd discovered at Saif's party to spend much time

reassuring the girl. His first impression had been of a quiet and contained young person, which had made the way she'd stood up to him all the more surprising. She'd showed no deference for his rank, or for that of his brother, and, in being completely open and frank, had opened his eyes to a world where women didn't simper and preen in the presence of immense wealth and power. If only she'd known it, Millie Dillinger had consigned every prospective bride of his to the remainder bin of history. None of them had her spirit.

Even though she'd been just fifteen, the connection between them had been immediate and strong, his overwhelming need to protect her his only concern. As he turned onto the corridor leading to what would be Tadj's suite, he thought back to his attempts to persuade Millie to leave the *Sapphire* for her own good, and her refusal to go without her mother. The child had become the carer, he'd thought at the time. She'd be twenty-three now, and had been an orphan for eight years, but, remembering the fire in those cornflower-blue eyes, he knew she was too strong for life to break her as it had broken her mother.

Wow! Quite literally: *wow!* Millie's jaw had dropped a little more with each step she'd taken on board the *Sapphire*, where every corner revealed a new wonder, but this guest suite was beyond belief. Ablaze with gold, it glowed with sapphires. Every surface that could be gilded was gilded, and every practical item, even down to the tiny waste-paper bin placed at one side of the solid-gold dressing table, was intricately worked, and

studded with precious stones. Striking works of art
hung on the walls, while soft furnishings begged to
be stroked and snuggled up to. Carpets and rugs? Oh,
yes. She was sinking in those up to her ankles. And
it was brilliantly lit. No dark corners here. No den of
vice. Miss Francine was right to say the *Sapphire* had
been completely transformed.

And now it was fit for a king, Millie thought as she
stood back to review her handiwork. Glancing in the
ornate mirror, she reassured herself that, in the un-
likely event that the laundress met a sheikh, the sheikh
wouldn't look twice at that laundress. In weather-
sensible shoes covered with blue plastic overshoes, an
old pair of jeans and a faded top, she'd come straight
from fixing a boiler, so although she'd washed her
hands until her skin had turned red she almost certainly still had the tang of oil about her.

Turning full circle, she tried to record every detail, so she could tell her friends when she got back
to the laundry. She had no doubt they would be in fits
of laughter when she told them about the erotic hangings above the bed. Though, in fairness, even the most
particular guest would be comfortable here. The suite
was definitely over the top, but it was also very airy
and welcoming. She had to admit, she was impressed.

The guard and the steward had remained outside
the door while Millie was working, so she could touch
this…lift that…peer behind the curtain at the elegant
balcony lit by the warm glow of a lantern—gold, of
course—and even quietly open the drawers… There

was nothing in them. She hadn't expected there to be, but couldn't resist having a nosey. Unlatching the door to the balcony, she stepped outside. Leaning over the railings, she wondered if her mother had stood here, and had maybe fallen from this very spot. It was possible...

Remaining quite still, almost as if she expected an other-worldly voice to fill in the details, she was finally forced to give up and return inside.

There was nothing sinister about this room, Millie told herself firmly. It smelled lovely, felt lovely, *was* lovely, apart from the lurid hangings. Could people really contort their bodies like that? Angling her chin, she tried to work out the mish-mash of limbs and faces, and had to give up. Anyway, the stateroom looked fabulous with those golden sheets in their rightful place. But who would sleep here? she wondered with a frown. Was this a gilded cage, waiting for another broken bird?

Stop it! This was a particularly lavish suite on board a billionaire's yacht, and nothing more. Millie had merely provided some final touches for a guest—

Khalid's mistress?

Why should she care? He might be married, for all she knew—

'Mademoiselle Millie?'

She almost jumped out of her skin as the door opened, but it was only the steward wanting to know if she needed any help. 'I'm doing fine, thank you,' she reassured him with a smile. 'I've nearly finished.'

Aladdin's cave could take another pop of gold, Millie concluded as the door closed quietly behind the

steward. And her overactive imagination could take a
hike. The Sheikh probably wasn't even on board. And
even if he were, would he have changed that much?
He was probably the same, devastatingly good-looking
charmer who made promises he couldn't keep; a man
who'd spirited his brother out of the country after her
mother's death.

Power and money made anything possible, Millie
concluded, firming her lips into an angry line. Eight
years ago, the headlines had read: 'The Nightingale
of London found drowned in King's Dock.' But had
her mother drowned? Or was she murdered? And did
anyone care?

Millie cared, and was determined to uncover the
truth of a night she would never forget. She wouldn't
rest until she found justice for her mother. Cause of
death had never been established, let alone convinc-
ingly explained to Millie. It felt to her as if everything had been brushed under the carpet. Claiming
diplomatic immunity, Sheikh Saif had left the country,
while his brother, now Sheikh Khalid, had remained
in the UK to clear up his mess. As far as Millie was
concerned, he was responsible for allowing Saif to get
away. The coroner's court had managed to establish
that drink and drugs had contributed to her mother's
drowning, but who had given her those things? Miss
Francine had warned Millie to leave the past alone,
but how could she ignore a chance like this? Sitting
down at the dressing table, she plucked the pencil out
of her hair and began to write a note on the order pad
she always carried.

She flinched guiltily as the door opened a second time, and stood, as if to demonstrate her readiness to leave. The guard was talking into his mouthpiece.

'Just collecting up my things,' she said.

If he noticed that she was nowhere by the bed, he didn't respond. He was too busy talking to whoever was at the other end of the line. She relaxed as he left the room. Maybe now she could finish that note.

Maybe not. The door opened again almost immediately.

He deplored ostentation. Even the intricately decorated solid-gold handle of this guest stateroom jarred as he closed his fist around it, but this particular suite of rooms had been kept intact, and was in the traditionally ornate style, favoured by his late brother. It served as a reminder to Khalid that extreme wealth could be extremely corrupting. He thought Tadj would appreciate the irony. The last time they'd stayed together had been in a basic tent when they were both serving in Special Forces.

After his brother's death, Khalid had insisted on a deep clean of the entire vessel, following which he'd brought in several cutting-edge designers to modernise the ship, with the proviso that this vintage suite be left intact. The best palace craftsmen had worked on the project, and the suite had fast become a talking point, both for its recording of unique and authentic historical detail, and for the erotic hangings above the bed.

'Your Majesty...'

He thought his guard seemed slightly uncomfortable. 'Yes?' Khalid paused with his hand on the door.

'I didn't expect you here so soon,' the guard admitted.

Khalid was instantly suspicious. 'Well, I'm here,' he said, opening the door wide.

'Millie?'

He would have known her anywhere, even after all this time. Eight years simply faded away. She'd changed beyond recognition, but the bond between them remained the same. She was a very beautiful woman. The braids were gone, likewise the spectacles, and there was no panic in her steady stare, reassuring him that her vibrant spirit was intact too.

The girl on the dock. Of course!

'Your Majesty!'

She seemed equally surprised, and for a few moments they just stared at each other. Her long, honey-gold hair was still damp from the rain where her oilskins had failed to protect her. Bundled up loosely on top of her head, the messy arrangement boasted an unusual ornament in the shape of a pencil, which she'd just stabbed into it as she catapulted away from the dressing table to stand in front of him, in what he guessed was the best expression of innocence she could muster. 'What are you doing?' he asked.

'Writing you a note,' she said with the frankness he remembered from all those years ago. 'I suppose I don't have to now,' she added.

'A note?' he queried.

'A request to meet with you—to talk,' she explained.

The bright blue eyes were completely steady on his. Her gaze was as direct as ever.

'Hello, by the way,' she added, as if finally realising that this meeting was a bombshell for both of them.

'Do you generally wear a pencil in your hair?' he asked as her cheeks blazed red.

'It's useful for writing notes on how to fix boilers,' she said.

He waved away the guard and steward as they entered the room to see what all the fuss was about. 'Welcome on board the *Sapphire*, Miss Dillinger.'

Her look said clearly, I'm not a guest, and if it hadn't been for these wretched sheets, I wouldn't be here at all.

Electricity didn't just crackle in the air, it was bouncing back and forth between them. She was so shocked at seeing Sheikh Khalid again, and in flowing robes that made him look more intimidating than ever, she couldn't think straight. What annoyed her most of all was the fact that he'd thrown her to the point where she was quivering like a doe on heat, rather than standing her ground in front of him like a hard-working professional.

It was time to get real. This was not the tough guy in jeans who invaded her dreams most nights, but an all-powerful king in whose water-borne kingdom she was currently—well, if not a prisoner, at the very least, vulnerable, which was not a condition she ever flirted with. No one could call his brutal attraction charm. However divinely warm, clean and sexy the Sheikh might appear, he was in reality a granite-faced titan without a single decent bone in his body. He'd turned a blind eye when she'd begged him for help. So whatever *her* body thought of his blistering masculinity, Millie Dillinger remained unimpressed.

But…

Calm down and think. This was almost certainly the only chance she'd ever get to ask him about that night. Being as different from the women he must be used to as it was possible to be, with her no-make-up face and her long hair piled carelessly on top of her head—not to mention the pencil garnish—she doubted she was in any immediate danger.

'When will you have finished your work?' he asked with an edge of impatience, confirming her conclusion that she was not his ravishment of choice.

'I have finished, Your Majesty. Please call the laundry if you need anything more.'

'I'll be sure to tell my housekeeper what you advise,' he commented with withering amusement.

Fortunately, she'd always been able to take a joke, though the thought that he might have a sense of humour only made it worse. If he was actually human, how had he allowed her mother to die? Whatever he'd done or not done on that night, it had changed the course of Millie's life, and had tragically ended her mother's. She had to dip her head so he couldn't see her angry eyes.

They came from different worlds, Millie concluded. In her world, people were answerable for their actions, but in his, not so much.

* * *

This was no milksop princess with a desire to please him, Khalid concluded, but a very angry woman, who was different and intriguing. She made him want to fist that thick gold hair and draw back her head so he could taste her neck. The girlish figure was long gone and had been replaced by curves in all the right places. Her features were pale from lack of sun, but her complexion was flawless. 'We will talk,' he promised as his senses sharpened. 'And sooner rather than later.'

'We must,' she returned fiercely, clenching her fists, which were held stiffly at her side.

She'd had years to ponder what had happened that night, so her anger was excusable. The death of her mother was bad enough, but believing he was involved in some sort of cover-up must be a festering wound. It was a reasonable supposition, he conceded.

'It must have been hard for you to return to the *Sapphire.*'

'Ghosts?' she suggested with a level look.

'Memories,' he countered.

'Life goes on,' she said flatly.

'As it must,' he agreed.

'Forgive me, Your Majesty, but if you don't have time to meet with me now, I have work to do on shore.'

She was dismissing him? he wondered with amusement.

'We're very busy at the laundry,' she excused, no doubt realising she had overstepped the mark.

On the contrary, he thought her a breath of fresh air. It would be all too easy for him to slip into the belief that because everyone else bowed the knee, Millie Dillinger would, or that other people's deference made him special in some way. A dose of Millie medicine was exactly what he needed. 'I will see you in my study in ten minutes' time.'

She seemed surprised and didn't answer right away. 'My time is also valuable, Ms Dillinger. My guard will escort you,' he explained, 'and my PA will call the laundry to explain your delay.'

'But—'

'Miss Francine is an intelligent woman,' he interrupted. 'She'll understand.'

Millie's frown deepened.

'Ten minutes,' he repeated before he left the room.

Millie wasn't sure she had breathed properly for the entirety of that interview. Sheikh Khalid was so much more than she remembered. She needed a big, wide space, and absolute silence to get used to it. And the guard didn't give her any time. He quick-marched her out of the sumptuous suite, and didn't pause until they stood in front of an impressive gleaming teak door. The entrance to the hawk's eyrie, Millie presumed. Squeezing her eyes tightly shut, she sucked in a deep, steadying breath, and prepared for round two.

At some silent signal, the guard deemed it appropriate to open the door. Standing back, he allowed her to enter. Sheikh Khalid was seated at the far end of his study behind a sleek modern desk where he appeared to be signing some documents. He didn't look up as she walked in. The scratch of his pen was a stark reminder that this was his territory, his kingdom, where things ran to his schedule, and she would have to wait until His Majesty was ready to receive her.

Forget pride. Any opportunity to interview a potential witness from that night had to be seized. She glanced around with interest. Order predominated. There was no clutter, no family photographs to soften the ambience—a fact that filled her with unreasonable relief—there was just a bank of tech and the desk piled high with official-looking documents.

Shouldn't he invite her to sit?

This might be the private space of a very private man, but Sheikh Khalid had invited her to come here. What about the so-called politeness of Princes? She'd explained that she was busy too. Ten minutes, he'd said. Did he time-keep to the second? That wasn't a bad thing, Millie counselled herself, because if Sheikh Khalid was so meticulous, he could hardly deny what he remembered of that night.

'My apologies,' he said at last, straightening up to fix her with his hawk-like stare. 'Millie,' he added softly.

His husky tone could have been a caress to her senses if she hadn't ruthlessly banished such nonsense in her thinking. 'That's right,' she said. 'We meet again.'

One ebony brow quirked, challenging her resistance to his blistering appeal. Their stares only had to connect for her body to respond with enthusiasm. Determinedly, she took an objective view. This study, this impersonal workspace, was deceiving. Designed to keep visitors at bay. She wasn't fooled. This was no cold, remote man who chose not to reveal his inner self, but a smouldering volcano, who surrounded himself with a sea of ice.

'You've been patient,' he commented with monumental understatement.

'For eight years,' she agreed.

They both knew that wasn't what he'd meant, and as they stared at each other across the desk she thought they were like two combatants facing each other across a ring.

CHAPTER FOUR

'ARE YOU SURE you wouldn't like to sit down?' the man she knew so well, and yet not at all, invited.

Sitting so he could tower over her was the last thing she wanted to do. 'If you're standing, I'm standing too,' she said as he left the desk. This seemed to amuse him. And he still towered over her. So be it. She had no intention of allowing His Majesty to win every point, even if her pulse was racing out of control.

'Forgive me for keeping you,' he added with a penetrating look. 'I have a lot of work.'

'So I see,' she replied calmly.

He studied her face. She studied him. Anything to take her mind off those mesmerising and all-seeing eyes. His headdress was called a keffiyeh. It moved fluidly as he moved, before falling back into place. She could try to be as objective as she liked, but when he angled his stubble-shaded chin to stare down at her, the lure of those eyes was irresistible, and as much as she wanted to hate him, the woman inside her wanted him more.

'And now I'm all yours,' he declared with the faintest of smiles.

She doubted that, and, for the sake of retaining her sanity, returned to studying his stylish robes. The keffiyeh was held in place by a rope-like *agal* made of tightly plaited gold thread that gave it the appearance of a crown. It could barely contain his wild hair, which was just as thick and black as she remembered, both from that night long ago, and from her forbidden dreams, when she had often run her fingers through those springing waves. Each time she woke when that happened, she was consumed by guilt.

How could she consider touching a member of the despised Khalifa family?

Just the thought made her angry. Yet here she was, standing in front of this same man with her body yearning for his touch.

'I don't have much time, Ms Dillinger,' he informed her sharply.

'And neither do I,' she replied, lifting her chin.

Calm. She must remain calm, Millie thought as his eyes drilled into hers. After Saif's profligate reign, she could understand that Sheikh Khalid was in a race against time to both put things right, and keep things right in his country. But that didn't mean she had to cut him too much slack.

'It's been a long time, Millie,' he said as if they were the best of friends. Of course, he had no reason to resent her. She'd kept out of his life, and got on with her own. 'You've done well,' he remarked. 'Engineering, isn't it?'

That shocked her. How much did he know about her? The Sheikh of Khalifa would make it his business to know everything about the people he encountered, she reasoned. 'Marine engineering,' she confirmed in a tone that didn't invite further questions.

'You haven't strayed far from King's Dock.'

'Why would I?' snapped out of her before she had worked out whether he was stating a fact or asking a question. Either way, how and where she lived was none of his business. 'I owe Miss Francine a debt of gratitude I can never hope to repay. And I love her,' she added with some challenge in her tone.

Instead of taking offence, something mellowed in the Sheikh's eyes and, turning, he asked, 'Would you like a drink?'

'Yes, please.' She hadn't realised how dry her throat had become, and was half expecting him to suggest she get it herself, or, failing that, he might ring a bell and have a steward bring it for her. It was a pleasant surprise when he pressed a panel on the wall behind his desk to reveal a comprehensive wet bar. He poured two glasses of water and, when he held hers out, their fingers brushed and she inhaled swiftly.

'We need a lot more time than I can spare for you tonight,' he said, appearing not to notice her response. 'And I suggest you learn to relax and trust me.'

Trust him? Was he serious? They were a long way from that. Sheikh Khalid might be much older and more experienced, but she was not a fool, and would work on keeping a clear head. That was far more important than relaxing.

Try thinking clearly in front of all this darkly glittering glamour. How could she avoid noticing the sharp black stubble coating, not just his chin, but the thick column of his neck when he tipped his head back to drink. She could only imagine what he'd look like naked—

She had to stop that right now. Thoughts like that were dangerous and inappropriate.

'A refill?'

'Yes, please.'

Their fingers brushed a second time. He knew, she thought, and could sense her arousal as sweet clenches in secret places begged her to forget the past. It was almost a disappointment when he chose to put distance between them, by moving away to lean back against the wall.

'Why are you frowning?' he asked.

Was she? 'This meeting has obviously come as a big shock for me.'

He shrugged disbelievingly. 'And yet you must have volunteered to come on board with the laundry, and when I invited you to chat in my study, you accepted.'

She should have found a member of staff to question about that night. Why hadn't she?

It was too late to wish she'd played this differently, Millie concluded. So, what now? How would it end? She shivered involuntarily. There was something in Sheikh Khalid's eyes that stripped her bare, right down to the depths of her soul.

He had been forced to put distance between them. Millie's allure was like an atomic charge to his senses. All he could think about was taking her over his desk... parting her legs and bringing her the release the hunger in her eyes said she so badly needed. Pressing her down beneath him, hearing her whimper with pleasure when he cupped her, worked her, before stripping her, so he could press his hard frame against her yielding softness—

He refused to submit to such carnal urges. Millie might be a beautiful woman, and the bond between them might have strengthened beyond belief, but the desire to protect her was intact. As was the desire to soften that stubborn mouth and turn her limbs languid with contentment. He was a stranger to hesitation and yet found himself contemplating a lengthy seduction, when what he should be doing was sending Millie back to the laundry without delay. It would be kinder for her. He must concentrate on choosing a bride, not a mistress.

But there was a yawning gulf between right and desire. 'Please,' he invited, indicating the chair opposite his at the desk. 'Why don't we both sit down and make the most of this short interview?'

Reluctantly, Millie sat down. I can handle this, she told herself firmly, but when the Sheikh sat across from her and steepled his lean, tanned fingers her mind was full of sex. She blamed the erotic images hanging on the wall in the gilded stateroom.

There was no one to blame but herself, and she'd feel worse if she didn't confront him with the real reason she was here. 'I want to know what happened that night,' she said. 'After I left the *Sapphire*, what happened?'

The Sheikh stared at her without speaking until all the tiny hairs on the back of her neck prickled. And then, instead of answering her question, he stood and came around the desk.

'What makes you think I saw what happened?' he demanded softly. 'I could have heard about the accident second-hand.'

'Accident?' Bridling, Millie shot to her feet.

'The coroner's court agreed with that supposition,' the Sheikh pointed out calmly, in no way rattled by her response.

'And closed the case,' she agreed, angrily clenching her fists. 'Does that seem fair to you?'

'I saw no reason to argue with the coroner's verdict.'

'I'm sure you didn't,' she said with a bitter laugh. 'But even if you didn't see what happened, I hope you're not asking me to believe that you never once questioned your brother.'

'We didn't share the close relationship you seem to imagine.'

'Even so, that's no excuse.'

She couldn't keep calm. She'd tried. And failed. This meeting could only play out as she'd planned if emotion could be kept out of it. And how could that happen now she'd plunged back into all the grief and guilt of learning about her mother's death?

In danger of wasting questions, she was also in danger of wasting precious time, but what would it take for Sheikh Khalid to tell her the truth? She had to find a way to make him, though dredging up the past would be the last thing he'd want to do.

She resorted to pleading. 'Can't you tell me anything?'

'Nothing you'd want to hear,' he said.

'Try me,' she said tensely. 'I know my mother had a problem with drink, and wasn't always responsible for her actions—that's why I asked you to go back and bring her out.'

'And if she didn't want to leave?' he asked evenly, keeping her locked in his stare.

'Surely, you could have done something? Or was my mother such an entertaining sight, you laughed along with everyone else?'

The Sheikh's expression turned stony. 'I hope you know that's not true.'

'How do I know anything?' Millie demanded heatedly. 'You won't tell me what happened. And now you're going to send me away without answers.'

'I sent you away that night for your own safety.'

'And then you broke your word,' she said bitterly.

'You don't know me and yet you judge me,' he said in a quiet and unnerving tone. 'You surely can't imagine I condone what happened on board the *Sapphire* that night?'

'I don't know. I don't know you!' Millie exclaimed, all the calm reserve that had kept her safe for all these years, deserting her completely. Its place was soon taken by drowning grief and corrosive guilt at the thought that, fifteen years old or not, *she* should have done something more to help her mother.

'Calm down,' the Sheikh advised as she clenched her jaw and wrung her hands.

This had the opposite effect. When he took hold of her shoulders, she shook him off angrily. 'Don't you dare tell me how to feel!' she raged as the emotion that had been bottled up for eight years erupted in fury. That terrible night could not be changed, and it was all coming back to her in vivid detail, and he was part of it.

'What are you doing?' she protested as he bound her close. 'Let go of me this instant!'

'I'm keeping you safe,' he ground out, his minty breath warming her face.

'So, I'm your captive now?' she derided. 'If you think you can keep me, as your brother would have kept my mother—?'

'Your imagination does you credit,' he said in an annoyingly calm tone, without making the slightest concession when it came to letting her go. 'I would remind you that your mother remained on board the *Sapphire* of her own free will.'

I don't want to hear this!

'And you can leave any time you like,' he added in that same maddening voice.

'All right—I will!'

It was surprisingly easy to break away. The Sheikh simply lifted his hands and let her go. And now she thought she must be going crazy to miss feeling safe in his arms. He'd made her feel safe that night eight years ago, and look what had happened then!

'I hate you!' she exclaimed.

'No, you don't,' he said. 'You're bewildered by the power of your emotions, and by the fact that you can't change anything about that night. You hate yourself, and there's no reason why you should.'

Burying her face in her hands, she accepted that he was right. She would never forget the morning after the party. She hadn't heard the news and had taken the bus to the marina to search for her mother. Determined to board the Sheikh's yacht, she had been all fired up. The bus had stopped short of the dock, and the driver had apologised, saying he couldn't take his passengers any further as there were ambulances and police tape in his way.

She'd known then. She'd felt the disaster like a cold, numbing mist that crept up from her feet until it took over her entire body. Miss Francine had been waiting outside the laundry. Ushering Millie inside, she had plied her with a cup of hot, sweet tea, before confirming the awful truth.

She must have been quiet, thinking about this for quite some time, Millie realised as she slowly became aware of the Sheikh staring down with concern. How dared he care about her now? His concern came too late. But instead of resisting his dark, compelling stare, she met it and felt tremors of awareness run up and down her spine.

'I'm sorry, Millie,' he said softly.

'Are you? Do you care?'

'You won't do anything silly when you leave here, will you?' he said without answering her question.

'Like my mother?' she suggested.

'Every story has more than one viewpoint,' he observed.

Lifting her chin, she gave it to him with both barrels. 'In this instance, a viewpoint that's convenient for you, and another that's not so convenient?'

His stare hardened again. 'That's your interpretation.'

Maybe, but Millie's vision encompassed the Sheikh striding back on board the *Sapphire* just before the royal limousine taking her home had turned a corner and she hadn't been able to see him any more. She'd craned her neck for one last glimpse of the man in whom she'd placed her trust, believing he'd put everything right.

'I'm sorry to rush you,' that same man said now as he glanced at his state-of-the-art wristwatch. 'I have another appointment.'

Millie's cheeks blazed red as she followed his glance to the door. 'Of course.' Time up. And what had she achieved? Precisely nothing.

'I have a party to prepare for,' he explained. 'Why don't you come back?' he said, startling her with this suggestion. 'I'll make time to speak to you.'

A *party* on board the *Sapphire*? Just the word was enough to invoke terrible memories and make her stomach churn with dread. 'I won't take up any more of your time,' she said tensely, turning for the door.

'But we're not finished,' he said. 'If you come tonight we can talk.'

Was he mad? Was she? Attend *a party* on board the *Sapphire*? Why was she even hesitating? Obviously, she had to say no.

'Thank you,' she said. 'What time shall I arrive?'

He shrugged. 'Any time after eight. It's a relaxed evening all across the ship. You might enjoy it.'

She might not.

'Until tonight,' he said before she had chance to change her mind.

'Until tonight,' she echoed. Something made her turn at the door, hoping this was her last big mistake. Staring into the Sheikh's knowing eyes was as dangerous as staring at the sun.

Dismissing his staff, he took the unusual step of personally escorting Millie off the ship. It was a reminder of why she was branded on his mind and always would be. The past had locked them together in a troubling set of memories, and in spite of his words to Millie, he was in no hurry to see her go. They took the stairs. Having the two of them confined in the cab of an elevator would be far too much too soon. However much he wanted to protect this new, older Millie, he wanted to seduce her more. They chatted politely about this and that as they walked through the *Sapphire* like two strangers who'd only just met. There wasn't just one elephant in the room, but two. Sex and death were a potent combination, and all that was needed for him to see her again.

'You're happy living above the laundry?' he asked.

'Of course I am,' she declared with a frowning, sideways look. And that was all she was going to say on that subject, he guessed, until they met later, when he was determined to find out more.

'How do you know where I live?' she asked.

He cursed himself for his carelessness. 'I presumed,' he fudged.

'The same way you know I'm studying engineering?' she queried. 'Should I be flattered by your
interest, or accept that a man like you must know everything about people you meet?

'Whichever,' she added with a shrug. 'I'll just mention that you seem to have more insight into my life
than I had expected.'

Was the Sheikh having her watched? Millie wondered.
If so, why? And how long had it been going on? Did
he think *she* knew something about that night—some
fact or gossip, or perhaps a careless remark made by
one of his crew when they were on shore?

It was a relief to step out on deck. Being too close
to a man like the Sheikh was unnerving. And exciting.
It was as if she had been plugged into a power source.
And that was dangerous, Millie concluded. No one
with any sense played with fire.

'I imagine your engineering skills must be very
useful to Miss Francine,' he remarked as they stood
in that awkward moment before parting.

Awkward for her, at least, Millie concluded. Once
again, he seemed frighteningly composed. While her
mind had just clicked into gear. 'You remember the
name of the laundry and its owner after all these years?'

'Your trolley?' he said, tamping down on a smile.
'Until later, Millie.'

'Yes,' she murmured distractedly, already having second thoughts. There was something not right about this.

'Don't forget you're coming back.'

'How could I forget?' she called back, subduing the brief spike of panic. She might not have achieved her goal to learn more about that night yet, but the Sheikh had given her a second chance. She had no idea what to expect at his party, but she wasn't a teenager now and could handle it.

What if the Sapphire *slipped its moorings and sailed away?*

She'd reach for her mobile phone and call the coastguard. She wasn't an impressionable teen, but a soon-to-be successful woman who decided her own fate.

The security guard had brought her roll-along bag dockside and she followed him without a backward glance. But once outside the dock gates, she paused and turned, to see the Sheikh still on deck, watching her.

'Until tonight,' he called out, raising a relaxed hand.

Decision time. Bottle out, or opt in. Her choice. 'Until tonight,' she yelled back.

CHAPTER FIVE

THERE WAS UPROAR at the laundry when Millie got back. Everyone wanted to know why she'd been delayed. Miss Francine hovered anxiously while the younger women clustered around Millie with endless questions, outrageous suggestions, and raucous laughter, as well as enough racy jokes to fill the playbill at a comedy show for a week.

Before she said anything, Millie brushed the hair out of her eyes and shed her oilskins. Hanging them up on the peg by the door, she grimaced. 'I'm drenched.'

'With passion?' Lucy suggested, nudging her closest companion.

For the sake of good humour, Millie adopted a mock aloof air. 'I hardly think the Sheikh invited me back tonight so he can seduce me.'

'He invited you back!' Lucy shrieked with a meaningful look at their colleagues.

'Out of politeness,' Millie insisted, catching Miss Francine's attention to reassure her with a look that Millie was okay with this comedy sketch. 'Something about making up the numbers,' she said vaguely.

'At the ruler of Khalifa's party?' Lucy exclaimed with obvious disbelief. 'You don't expect us to believe he left something like that to chance, do you?' she demanded with an eye roll.

'I'm just not seduction material,' Millie insisted, turning serious. At least that much was true. Her mother's looks might have been ravished by pain and abuse, but Roxy Dillinger had always been beautiful, while Millie made the best of what she'd got, which wasn't much. But what she lacked in kerb appeal, she tried to make up for with zest for life.

A barrage of questions about her time on the *Sapphire* hit her from every side. What was the Sheikh like? What was it like on a billionaire sheikh's superyacht? Editing heavily, Millie gave as full an account as she could.

'Why you Millie?' Lucy demanded in a teasing tone. 'What have you got that the rest of us lack?'

'The rest of you have got too much work to do, to be gossiping like this,' Miss Francine insisted above a chorus of groans. 'We'll have our own party when the work's completed,' she promised to a second chorus, this time of cheers.

'I'd rather be Millie,' Lucy called out cheerfully as she got back to her work.

Everyone took the hint and got their heads down, though Millie still had to field a whole host of questions, as well as the teasing remarks of her co-workers, but it had the good effect of making time fly. Good for everyone, Millie concluded, but herself, as, before she knew it, work ended and she had to get ready for the party. Suddenly, she didn't feel so brave.

Don't be such a *wuss*, she told herself impatiently as she ran up the stairs to her cosy bedsit. She had no excuse not to know how fast things could change from hope to tragedy. She had to seize the moment and make the most of it.

Relax. Chill, Millie mused, eyes tightly shut as she stood beneath the shower. If she didn't take this chance to find out the truth about that night, she'd spend the rest of her life wishing she had.

What to wear to a billionaire's party when you wanted to blend into the crowd? That was the burning question. Millie should have asked about the dress code, she realised now. Sheikh Khalid had mentioned something about a casual evening. Good. Casual she could do. An apprentice engineer had more overalls in her closet than frocks, but she did have one nice dress.

It was red, which was unfortunate. Would it make her stand out too much? She didn't want to look as if she'd tried too hard. She'd bought it in the sales, thinking it perfect for the next Christmas party. At least it was an unfussy style, just a simple column of bright red silk. Having made her decision, she hung the dress on the back of the door.

Hair up or down? She'd tie it back, Millie decided. Tossing her long, honey-gold hair for effect wasn't her style. Having trialled a few different looks, she settled on her customary messy up-do. She'd got the knack of arranging that now, but she swopped out the infamous pencil for a simple mock tortoiseshell clip.

Shoes?

Wearing high heels on a ship grated, somehow. She compromised with a strappy flat.

Underwear. She rootled through her drawer. Sensible big knickers, obviously...

So why was she holding a flimsy thong?

Who was going to see what she wore? No one. So she settled for the thong. It wouldn't show any lines beneath the dress.

As she got ready she kept on glancing out of the window to where the *Sapphire* was berthed and blazing with light. When she'd finished she leaned back against the wall, eyes closed, trying to blot out that other party and replace it with the new. If she didn't, she'd never have the courage to step back on board the *Sapphire*.

Music from the superyacht wafted over the marina and into Millie's bedroom. It was tasteful, tuneful music. She'd be all right. She had to be. No one could pick up the pieces. She had to do that for herself, and owed it to her mother to move forward, which was exactly what she intended to do.

Checking her appearance in the mirror one last time, she declared, 'No problem. I'm ready to enter the lion's den.'

Khalid frowned as he paced the deck. The band was playing, and his stewards were putting the final touches to place settings as his guests began to arrive, but there was no sign of Millie. He wanted to see her. They had a lot to discuss.

Discuss?

All right, he snarled at his moral compass director, but she'd be here. She wouldn't be able to resist what might be her last chance to question him, and, if the temptation to interrogate him wasn't enough, he had to trust that the same primal energy drove both of them, and that was an irresistible force.

An eclectic mix of specialists from the arts, sciences, and the charities he supported, as well as tech kings and a few fellow royals, had gathered on the deck below his quarters. It was an interesting crowd. He was keen for her to see the changes his rule had brought about. It had always been important for him to draw a clean line between the way his brother Saif had ruled, and his own very different approach. Had he mentioned the dress code for her evening would be casual? He couldn't believe he was worrying about something so trivial, but he wanted Millie to fit in and relax, and if she arrived in a ball gown—She wouldn't arrive in a ball gown. She had more sense. There was more risk she'd arrive straight from work in a boiler suit smeared with oil.

'Your Majesty seems particularly distracted tonight—'

'Tadj!' He whirled around to greet his friend. 'Forgive me. I didn't see you and your companion arrive. Good evening, Ms…?'

'Lucy Gillingham, Your Majesty. I work at Miss Francine's with Millie.'

'No need to curtsey,' he said, raising Lucy to her feet with a smile. 'Welcome on board the *Sapphire*.'

'It must be a very beautiful woman to distract you to this extent,' Tadj teased him discreetly. 'May I ask who she is?'

'No. You may not,' he told Tadj. 'Your reputation goes before you, my friend.' He had no intention of sharing his interest in Millie with a man known as the Wolf of the Desert for a very good reason.

'The party's already a success,' Tadj observed, glancing down to where the good-natured throng was mingling easily.

'Seems so,' Khalid agreed, scanning the crowd for Millie. 'Excuse me—I can see some more guests arriving—'

'A *very* beautiful woman,' Tadj called after him with amusement, no doubt having spotted where Khalid was heading.

Millie was trying to find her way through the crowd jostling around his stewards as they offered his guests a welcoming flute of champagne. She looked sensational in a slender column of bright red silk. The crowd parted for him, so he quickly reached her side. 'You decided to come?' he remarked.

Running her eyes over him from top to toe, she looked up and smiled. 'It appears so, Your Majesty.'

'Have you been practising?' he asked with amusement as she attempted to bob a curtsey.

'Only as much as you've been working on your boilers today,' she countered, directing this into his eyes as she straightened up. 'Actually, I'd love to see the engine room.'

'Another time,' he said.

'You're inviting me back?' she challenged with amusement. 'I would have thought you'd seen enough of me by now.'

'By the end of the evening, I probably will have done,' he replied in the closest to humour he intended to come. In truth, he couldn't wait to get away from her. She was affecting him like no aphrodisiac known to man.

'I imagined you'd be leaving soon?' she said, clearly unaware of his physical discomfort.

A flowing robe would have been more accommodating than designer jeans, he acknowledged, masking his discomfort. 'And so I shall. My work is done,' he confirmed, sounding harsher than he'd intended, but the need to rearrange himself was becoming more pressing by the moment.

I will not allow myself to be distracted by a pair of knowing black eyes, Millie determined. And if Khalid thought he could just walk away from her, he was wrong. 'I find older vessels fascinating,' she said, determined to keep him in front of her. 'So much experience under their belt.'

He actually groaned as if he were in pain. 'I hope you're not referring to me?'

His voice sounded strangled, but if that was an attempt at humour, it saved him. He might actually be human. 'I hardly think so, Your Majesty.'

People were watching them with interest, she noticed. Gossip would spread quickly on the marina. The ruler of Khalifa and a local laundress, chatting together like old friends. She didn't care, but did he? And if he did care, he might bring this to an end at any moment, before they had chance to arrange that private talk. 'You invited me here to talk,' she said. 'When can we do that?'

'I need time with my guests. At least an hour.'

'Of course,' Millie agreed promptly. 'And my apologies if I'm keeping you.'

'I choose to talk to you.'

And when you no longer choose to do so, you'll move on, she thought. Determined to pin him down, she confirmed, 'An hour. Where?'

'I'll send someone to find you.'

'Do you delegate everything to someone else?'

The words just popped out of her mouth, and there was a moment when she thought he wouldn't answer, but then he said, 'Not all things, Ms Dillinger.'

And now she really, *really* wished she hadn't asked the question, as the expression in the Sheikh's eyes took hold of every nerve-ending in her body and rattled it until it squeaked.

'Don't worry about me,' she said on a dry throat. 'I'm happy people-watching, just so long as we have that promised talk.'

'I won't forget,' he said in a way that left her in no doubt that he meant it.

'Okay.' She shrugged and smiled politely as he left.

That shrug. That smile.

Millie's wildflower scent taunted his senses as he walked away.

It stayed with him—*she* stayed with him as he met and chatted to his guests. To a casual observer, the ruler of Khalifa had been exchanging small talk with a beautiful local woman who had happened to catch his attention. There was nothing unusual about that. On the surface, maybe, but beneath the apparent calm there was a lot more going on, like a fault line in the ocean with a volcano simmering underneath.

She needed a lot more time to relax on the *Sapphire*. Being back here was upsetting, and disturbing, Millie thought as Sheikh Khalid walked away. Needing something to take her mind off the past, she began to circulate and introduce herself around. She might have worried that she was walking in her mother's footsteps, if the guests at this party hadn't been so very different from those of eight years ago. Millie gave no explanations and none were needed, other than the fact that she lived locally, as the Sheikh was a generous host and had invited people from all walks of life. His guests were so open and pleasant that for a while she lost herself in conversation, but revisiting the place where she'd last seen her mother alive had affected her more than she'd thought.

She kept hearing her mother's last words ringing in her head. *'Get her out of here! You're nothing but a little killjoy. You always spoil my fun!'*

Her mother had been a victim and Millie was anything but, she reasoned, and she had to be strong for both of them. But that wasn't easy when her feelings were in turmoil, and the past kept rolling over her like a storm that threatened to engulf her in grief and guilt. The Sheikh had the knack of putting everyone at ease, she noticed. She also couldn't help noticing that he looked amazing. He had no need of royal robes to point up his blistering masculinity. Dressed casually in jeans and a shirt, he was every fantasy hero made real. Tall, tanned, hard-muscled and obviously super-fit, he radiated undeniably compelling sex appeal.

The biggest shock of all came when she bumped into her friend Lucy. It was a double shock to identify Lucy's stunningly good-looking companion.

'Isn't he gorgeous?' Lucy exclaimed as they hugged.

'You're on a date with the Emir?' Millie whispered back.

'Don't sound so alarmed. We met dockside. He's a man, I'm a woman. What's wrong with that?' Everything and nothing, Millie thought as Lucy added, 'How are you and the Sheikh getting on?'

'There is no me and the Sheikh. I already told you, I'm here to make up the numbers and nothing more.'

As if sensing their interest in him, Khalid, who was some distance away, turned to look at Millie and frowned. If she didn't know better, she'd think he was surprised to see her at the party. Was she supposed to go home until the hour was up and then come back? He'd invited her, and she'd rather be here, dicing with danger, than fretting about all the questions she wanted to ask him, back at home.

'He shouldn't be allowed to wear robes—'

'Sorry?' She glanced at Lucy, who had been having a one-sided conversation, Millie realised now.

'The robes?' Lucy pressed. 'They hide his body. Sheikh Khalid owes it to the world to only ever wear snug-fitting clothes, like the ones he's wearing now.'

'Oh, yes,' Millie said vaguely.

'You're not listening, are you?' Lucy teased. 'What's a nice girl doing staring at the Sheikh?'

'I'm not staring at the Sheikh,' Millie defended. 'It's what's inside the package,' she murmured distractedly.

'Depends on the package,' Lucy put in. 'Personally, I can't wait to unwrap Tadj.'

They said laughing goodbyes, and as Lucy walked off Millie reassured herself that they could both look after themselves, even in the company of these devastating-looking men.

'Are you ready to talk now?'

She almost jumped out of her skin, hearing Khalid's voice so close behind her.

She could handle this.

'Has an hour passed already?' she asked lamely as his heat invaded every inch of her body.

'I thought you would have been eating by now.'

'But…' She looked at the dining table and frowned. His guests were only just sitting down. 'The canapés did look delicious,' she admitted, thinking he must mean the trays of bite-sized appetisers the stewards had been handing round, 'but I didn't want to spoil my dinner.'

'Quite right,' he said, but now it was the Sheikh's turn to frown.

What was going on? He'd invited her to supper.

Leading the way through his guests, he greeted everyone who wanted to speak to him. He even introduced Millie as an old friend. *An old friend?* she thought as they mounted the companionway to a higher deck.

'It's a beautiful night,' he remarked as he paused at the top.

It was. The rain had cleared, and it was crisp and clear with stars glittering overhead. A magical night, Millie thought.

And on just such a night, her mother had drowned in this same marina.

'I want to show you something,' he said, distracting her before that thought had a chance to take hold. A dart of apprehension still struck her hard. Maybe it was his tone of voice. Following him to the stern, she followed his stare and frowned. 'A lifeboat?' she queried.

'This is the last place I saw your mother alive.'

Millie's fingers tightened on the cold, steel rail. She must compose herself, and must do so fast, or lose any hope she had of getting to the bottom of this.

'Are you okay?' the Sheikh asked.

'Yes,' she managed in a clipped tone. She didn't trust herself to say anything more. 'What was my mother doing here in a lifeboat?'

'Sleeping,' he said.

Sleeping it off, Millie thought, but she was glad he hadn't said that. It hurt to hear her mother criticised, even now. Her mother deserved respect, though she'd had none for herself.

'You let her sleep?' she said, trying to get a picture of what had happened that night.

'But with a guard watching over her,' he said.

'What happened next? What went wrong?' she pressed. 'You said she slipped away. Didn't anyone miss her? What about your brother? Wasn't he expecting my mother to sing for his guests?'

'My brother—'

'Your brother *what*?' she cut in impatiently, unable to hold back as her emotions surged out of control.

'I can't answer for my brother's whereabouts at each precise moment during that night.'

'You must have some idea,' she insisted. 'And if you can't tell me, I don't know why I'm here—'

The shock when he seized hold of her arm, as she was about to walk off, flashed through her like a lightning bolt. 'Let go of me!' Wrenching her arm out of his grip almost threw her off balance, and she had to hold onto the rail with both hands to steady herself. It felt cold and as unyielding as he was. How he had to be, she thought. He'd had to handle the authorities at the time, and give his lawyers a story they could run with. He was hardly going to tell her another story now.

But still she wondered… *Did my mother touch this rail? Did she cling to it and try to save her life?*

'Did she fall here?' she asked at last. She turned to face him, her grim expression demanding the truth.

'Your mother had had too much to drink. I was surprised she was even capable of moving.'

'Something must have prompted her to climb out of the lifeboat.' Millie shook her head. 'It had to be something so urgent she found the strength.' She glanced over the rail, and her head swam as her imagination supplied the detail: the scream, the splash, the struggle, and finally silence.

'No.'

She was so wrapped up in her thoughts, she barely heard the single word, and only slowly turned to face the Sheikh. 'There's something you're not telling me,' she said.

'This has been a shock for you.'

'That's no answer,' she said tensely.

Happy sounds from the party rose all around them, mocking her state of mind. This was bizarre, tense and horrible. Learning details about that night, while she was battling feelings she shouldn't even have for this man, left her swamped in sadness and tortured by guilt. She couldn't stop thinking that if only she'd been older and more authoritative at the time of her mother's death, maybe she could have saved her.

'My brother could always find women to entertain him,' Sheikh Khalid was saying. 'It's not surprising that he lost interest in your mother's whereabouts.'

'As you did,' she flared.

'I put guards on watch,' he reminded her.

'They couldn't have been much good,' she observed acidly.

'Your mother asked to use the facilities, and of course they let her go.'

'In a drunken state on board a yacht without following her?' Millie exclaimed. 'That sounds like gross dereliction of duty to me.'

'You weren't there,' the Sheikh interrupted. 'There- fore, you're in no position to pass judgement on my staff. I'm satisfied they did all they could.'

'How can you say that?' Millie demanded hotly. 'I've been followed every step of the way since I boarded the *Sapphire*, yet you're asking me to believe my mother could wander at will.'

'As I've tried to explain, times were different, and there were no witnesses.'

'But someone must have seen something,' she in- sisted.

Ignoring her interruption, the Sheikh continued. 'I was clearing the grand salon at the time of your moth- er's disappearance. Saif had tried to have me thrown off the *Sapphire*, but his guards had refused to do this. They supported me rather than my brother, though even with their help it still took time for all the guests to leave. As soon as I was free, I went to look for your mother. I wondered at first if she'd returned to my brother, but his attendants hadn't seen her. I can only conclude she slipped away with the rest of the guests leaving the ship.'

'So, you're saying your brother had nothing to do with my mother's death.'

'That's what I told the authorities.'

That's no answer, she thought. 'I can see it would be convenient for you to hear nothing and see nothing.'

'Have you finished?' he asked coldly.

'Why? Are you going to have me drummed off the ship?'

'No part of this tragedy could ever be described as convenient,' the Sheikh assured her.

'For your brother, then,' Millie said.

'My brother's dead.'

'And does that absolve him from blame? If you're saying he deserves respect, simply because he's no longer with us, then so does my mother. And you might as well know, I intend to clear her name—'

'That's as it should be,' he said.

'What's the point in talking further?' Millie asked. 'You're not going to tell me anything.'

'You're leaving?'

She'd thought about it. 'No,' she said, 'not unless you have me thrown off. Eight years ago my mother had no one to protect her, but now she does, and I'm not a biddable teenager who'll go home when she's told.'

'You have always defended her,' he said with the closest to admiration he'd come yet.

'I trusted you,' she said quietly. Lose her temper lose the battle, Miss Francine had always said, and the *Sapphire* provided valuable business for the laundry. Millie must manage her quest for justice and look at the bigger picture.

They stared at each other unblinking for a few moments, which was as troubling as it was a sign of Millie's intent. Her determination to get to the bottom of the mystery surrounding her mother's death had crossed her path with that of a man whose potent persona was wreaking havoc on her control. There was no such thing as a meaningless glance where the Sheikh was concerned. He could convey more in a look than any book of words, and his dark eyes suggested an agreement of a very different kind, one that had no connection with the past, and everything to do with the here and now.

CHAPTER SIX

MILLIE WAS RIDICULOUSLY appealing and passions were high. Drawing her close, Khalid looped an arm around her waist and tipped up her chin until their mouths were only a hair's breadth apart.

'Don't you dare touch me,' she flared.

Her struggles only brought them closer. This first, real physical contact between them was an incendiary device to his senses. His greedy flesh was aroused to the point of agony. She rested, panting, for a moment, blazing her defiance into his eyes. A lithe young flame to his dark, smouldering passion, she was as much a slave as he to primitive forces that made her eyes shoot sparks of fury at him, even as they darkened.

'You're to blame for all of this!' she raged. Reaching up, she seized hold of his shoulders, which only brought them closer together.

He held her at arm's length. 'I think you're over-wrought.'

Savouring her fresh, clean scent while she vibrated with awareness beneath his hands, he thought, *Not yet.* She was all eagerness, and ready to channel her anger into a different sort of passion, but he favoured trial by frustration. Pleasure delayed was pleasure enhanced. She deserved nothing less.

He was actually considering seducing her?

Yes. It seemed inevitable, though his family had destroyed hers, and he had no doubt that coming back to the *Sapphire* and reliving that night had made her hate him. But hate was a strange and adaptable emotion. His desire to protect her was as strong as ever, but the desire to make love to her was even stronger, Millie's passion could change into something very different. Gently, but firmly, he removed her hands from his body and stepped back. He could not have predicted her reaction.

'Don't,' he rapped as she covered her face with her hands. 'You have nothing to feel guilty about.'

'Don't I?' she said bitterly, raising her chin. 'Not even when those feelings involve you?'

She shocked him with words that sounded wrenched from her soul. Her frankness had always been Millie's greatest appeal, he reminded himself as he observed, 'This has been an ordeal. You should go home now and rest. We'll speak on another occasion.'

'And if the *Sapphire* leaves?' she said, her eyes glaring into his.

'Go home, Millie.'

'Why should I make it easy for you?'

'Go home,' he repeated. 'I'll have one of my guards accompany you.'

She laughed at this. 'To make sure I'm safe?' she said. 'I think we can assume I know my own way home, and there's no need for you to have me escorted off the *Sapphire*.'

Her face was pale and defiant as they confronted each other. 'You're not being removed from the ship,' he stated evenly. 'It's dark, and I'm concerned about you. It can be dangerous on the dock.'

'As my mother discovered,' she agreed tensely.

'You will accept my guard,' he instructed quietly. 'He'll be discreet, and I won't argue about this. I insist.'

Her mouth flattened stubbornly, but she could see the sense in what he said, and eventually she grudgingly nodded her head. 'So, when will we talk?' she pressed. 'Or have you changed your mind about that.'

'I haven't changed my mind,' he said as he waved a guard over. 'Before I leave King's Dock we'll meet again and talk calmly. A party isn't a suitable venue for a discussion as weighty as ours.' He wanted her behind closed doors, to navigate both their feelings and the past.

She huffed a short, and, he thought, disbelieving laugh. 'Thank you, Your Majesty. Goodnight,' she added briskly.

When she extended her hand for him to shake, he took hold of it and brushed it with his lips, and felt her tremble. As he watched her walk away, he knew this wasn't over and that it had only just begun. His hunt for a bride would have to wait.

What the hell was I thinking going back on the *Sapphire* with some crazy notion to get in touch with the Sheikh?

Dropping down on her bed, Millie kicked off her shoes and sent them flying across the room. Instead of learning more about the night of her mother's death she had almost *kissed* her greatest enemy? What was that about? This was a man who must have lied to the police, and whose lawyers had glibly lied to the coroner, which had allowed his brother, the late Sheikh Saif, to leave the country without so much as having his wrist slapped.

Someone must pay for her mother's death. Was Millie supposed to believe that Roxy Dillinger had crawled out of a lifeboat dead drunk, used the facilities, as Sheikh Khalid had so tactfully put it, and then fallen into the sea? Had anyone seen this happen? What about security cameras? From what she'd seen when she was on board the *Sapphire*, the big ship was bristling with cameras. Someone had to know the truth. And that someone wasn't telling.

Springing up, she paced to the window and pushed back the blind. The *Sapphire* was even more awe-inspiring at night when it was lit up prow to stern. The classy party would last until the early hours of the morning, she guessed. It was certainly going full swing now. She could have kicked herself for not finding out when the *Sapphire* was due to leave King's Dock. It could slip away in the night while she was asleep, and she'd be none the wiser, and that would be her chance to discover the truth gone for ever.

And she might never see Sheikh Khalid again.
Good!
Not good. She'd miss him. Seeing him again had re-

ally affected her, Millie realised. She hadn't been exaggerating when she'd admitted having feelings for him.

Feelings? The heartache she was experiencing was a real physical pain.

Love hurt? You bet. Love for her mother and confusion where Sheikh Khalid was concerned. And she'd blown her one and only chance. Saying he'd make time to see her again was just a throw-away comment, a pleasantry, *the politeness of princes.*

Maybe, but she wasn't a quitter, so what to do now?

'Okay,' she informed the empty room. 'There's only one thing for it…'

Reaching under the bed for her shoes, she slipped them back on. Smoothing her hair, she glanced in the mirror. Drawing a deep breath, she announced, 'I can do this.' Turning for the door, she headed back to the party.

It was easy to convince the guard to let her pass through the locked gate guarding the *Sapphire*'s berth with nothing more than a smile and the truth. 'I left something at the party,' she explained. Well, she had, if you counted her heart and a whole pile of questions.

'No problem, Miss Dillinger,' the guard told her politely as he unlocked the steel gate and swung it wide.

She was checked a second time at the foot of the gangplank, and again at the entrance to the ship, by which time her pulse was going crazy. What would Khalid's reaction be when he saw her? Too late to worry about that now, Millie thought. She was here and she was going to go ahead with this.

She wasn't sure what made her glance up as she

waited for another tick to be placed against her name on yet another clipboard in the hands of a flint-faced guard. Was it animal instinct? An invisible bond? Or a silent whisper, she mused romantically, to take her mind off the compelling individual staring down in her direction.

'Come up,' Sheikh Khalid indicated with a jerk of his chin, before stepping back into the shadows behind the rail on the top deck.

Triumph surged through him as Millie boarded the *Sapphire*. He'd known she'd come back. He'd been waiting for her. She wasn't stupid. Millie knew there was something he hadn't told her and she couldn't take the chance he'd sail away. She wasn't here to sell herself for information. Millie wasn't like her mother with desperation as her only driver. She was a seeker of justice and truth, and she was principled. The urge to protect her was stronger than ever, as were his feelings of guilt. The chemistry between them was insane. Raw, physical hunger surged through his body, a warning to protect her from him, as well as the past. Whatever she was expecting him to tell her tonight, he would not destroy her with the truth. It was so much worse than she could imagine. Millie had forged a new life, and he was glad of it. There was nothing to be gained by making her look back at the past.

Millie was intuitive as well as beautiful, and she was right to come here tonight. As she had suspected, the *Sapphire* would be leaving King's Dock soon.

Spending these last few hours in her company would have to be enough. But as she ran up the companionway towards him, he thought there was only one way, a visceral way, to get Millie out of his system. Unfortunately, that was an indulgence he must deny himself. There were other pleasures to distract him. He'd been away from the desert too long. A Bedouin at heart, he would always be restless, and had never craved the challenge of his native land more.

When she appeared framed in the doorway, it was as if the air changed and freshened all around him. Waiting until her eyes had adjusted to the much dimmer lights on this deck, she appeared ethereal and vulnerable. He knew nothing could be further from the truth. Millie was no victim. She was very much together, and tonight determination showed in her expression as if she believed destiny was on her side.

'Over here,' he called out.

Her chin lifted and her gaze landed squarely on his face. His biggest problem was remembering she was innocent in all things, as a fierce carnal hunger did its best to wipe out his previous saintly thoughts.

I know what I'm doing, Millie intoned silently as the security guard who had accompanied her on board the *Sapphire* retreated and the door closed behind him with a soft click, leaving her on a deserted deck with only his most regal majesty, Sheikh Khalid of Khalifa, for company. Security had improved over the years, she'd noticed as she'd passed through the ship.

The party that she and her mother had attended had been a free-for-all, but tonight a good mix of people, who could enjoy themselves without getting drunk, were hosted and protected, rather than guarded, by the Sheikh's most excellent staff. But that didn't make her soften towards him. She would settle for nothing less than the truth. He could forget the edited version. Learning what had really happened that night was the only reason she was back here.

The only reason?

'Welcome,' he said.

As his husky and seductive tone took a leisurely stroll across her senses, she told herself firmly that Sheikh Khalid was nothing like his brother, and she was safe. Sheikh Khalid had let her mother down, but had saved Millie. Would he save her again by filling in those gaps that had lashed her with guilt for eight long years?

She was here in search of the truth, but also, Millie silently admitted as she raised her face to his, because she couldn't stay away. There was something between them that wouldn't allow her to. The *Sapphire* was in dock. Sheikh Khalid was close, and, as many times as she told herself that she couldn't miss this opportunity, it was far, *far* more than that. She couldn't breathe easy. She couldn't think straight. She couldn't function properly. Only when she knew everything would they part and go their separate ways.

And was that all it was?

That was all it could be, she told herself as his dark, all-seeing eyes drilled down into hers. What else could it be? Arousal, sadness, guilt and anger collided inside her, making her long and loathe, and feel a type of passion she had never experienced before. They had no future together. That was the bottom line. Even if she could get past her simmering suspicion that he could have done more to save her mother, they were worlds apart, with an unbridgeable gulf between them.

But as the Sheikh's confidence and sexual energy enveloped her in erotic heat, she became more confused than ever. He was so big, so brazenly masculine; in every way, he was different, and on a completely different scale from other men. She trembled with awareness of his brute strength. Sheikh Khalid had no need of royal robes to stamp him with the majesty of power. His authority was unparalleled. And there was a part of her, a reckless part, that wanted nothing more than to battle with him.

Go head to head, at least, she reasoned. That was why she was here, after all.

'We'll talk inside,' he said, leading the way into the shadows of his apartment on board the *Sapphire*.

She had started to follow, but for some reason stepped back instead of forward, and managed to trip over a cleat sticking up from the deck. His reflexes were lightning fast. Whirling around as she yelped and stumbled, he yanked her hard against his chest.

'Steady,' he murmured as their bodies collided.

It was a few moments before he released her, and she was in no hurry to move away. 'What do you really want?' he asked, staring deep into her eyes. 'What do you want of me, Millie Dillinger?'

Her only thought was, *You*. And the truth shocked her. She had been fighting her attraction to him since the moment they met again, Millie realised now, but this was something more, so much more. The worst of it was, he gave a smile as if he knew.

Freeing herself, she pulled away. At best he must think her gauche, and at worst he might think her her mother's daughter. Even in the middle of these two poles apart was a world of 'you're wasting the best chance you ever had to clear your mother's name'.

'I don't know what happened that night,' she said, feeling she must say something. 'But I can tell you this. My mother wasn't weak, she was desperate, and vulnerable, and your brother took advantage of that.'

'We need to talk,' the Sheikh told her in a calm, unthreatening voice.

'Too much has been brushed under the carpet,' she continued as soon as they were inside.

They were in a lovely room, she registered vaguely; it might have been called a snug in a cosy, suburban home, and was the first real sign that the imposing figure towering over her relaxed occasionally. Enough to tell her the truth? That remained to be seen.

'You seem so sure that things have been hidden from you,' he said, indicating that she should sit on one of the two facing sofas.

She remained standing. 'Wouldn't you?'

'Maybe you're overthinking things,' he suggested, staring down. 'And maybe you're not telling me all of the truth.'

Something flickered in his eyes, suggesting she'd hit the mark.

'And maybe I'm trying to protect you,' he countered softly.

'Perhaps that's what you'd like me to think.'

'You're beautiful.'

As he murmured this, she drew her head back and gave him one of her looks. 'I came here for a serious discussion.'

Which was true, but a thrill of excitement still ripped through her as the Sheikh's hard mouth tugged in the faintest of smiles. 'I'm being absolutely serious,' he assured her at the same mesmerising low volume.

There was a scar that cut down the side of his cheek to his mouth, she noticed now. His stubble usually covered it, but he must have shaved quite recently for the party. *Or for her?* The party, Millie told herself firmly as she progressed the thought; everyone had some sort of scar, it was just that some hid them better than others.

'We have all evening to talk,' he said with an easy shrug.

Talk, when she was drowning in testosterone?

Millie could have stepped away when he reached out to find the clip in her hair and release it, but she didn't, and long, silken skeins fell tumbling to her waist.

'Beautiful,' he whispered again as he tossed the clip aside. He combed his fingers through her hair, soothing and exciting her in turn, but she tossed her head, as if pleasure were a sin. 'Guilt?' he asked. 'Why, when you've no reason to feel guilty? Desire is a natural human emotion—'

'That I can resist,' she assured him as she stepped away.

He laughed softly and saw her hesitation. 'You have the same spirit I loved eight years ago.'

'Spirit prompted by my desperate concern for my mother,' she reminded him. 'You promised to go back on board and save her.'

'I did all I could,' he said steadily. Her voice was shaking with emotion. Too much had been bottled up inside Millie for too long. He could imagine the child growing to be a woman, and never once losing control, because if she did the grief would break her. He wanted to comfort her and make love to her all at one and the same time, but his self-control would not allow it.

'So, what do you want of me, Millie Dillinger?'

'I might ask you the same question,' she fired back with surprising passion.

That was it. The dam was breached. 'I want you,' he said.

Millie gasped. Sheikh Khalid wanted her. This was every dream come true, and every nightmare made real. Guilt and desire battled inside her. His grip was both gentle and firm. She wanted this, wanted him. He was holding her in front of him with a message in his eyes that even a relative innocent like Millie could not possibly misinterpret, and that message surged through her senses, urging her to act. He wanted her. She wanted him. As amazing as it seemed to someone whose sexual experience was limited to a few fumbles in the back of a car, Sheikh Khalid wanted to seduce her, and she wanted to be seduced. To be introduced to the world of sensuality she'd only dreamed about, by a man who could teach her everything, was—

Madness.

'I should go—'

'And find out nothing?' he said.

What was he talking about now? That night? Or sex? She shook her head, as if to shake some sense into it, but primal hunger was a merciless force. What harm could one night do? And once they were truly intimate who knew what she might learn?

I'm going to interrogate him as he seduces me? Did she seriously expect Sheikh Khalid to betray his brother?

'Well?' he prompted. 'Are you staying?'

'I think you underestimate me,' she said tensely.

'That's not an answer.' And then he laughed, a blaze of strong white teeth against his swarthy skin. 'I would never make that mistake, Millie, but I suspect you might.'

The Sheikh's face was dangerously close as he dipped his head. She didn't know what to expect and remained frozen as he brushed her lips with his. But frozen wasn't an option for more than a split second, as he tested and teased and made every atom in her being long for more.

She had thought she was stronger than this, but she had never encountered a force of nature like Khalid before. From teasing, he moved seamlessly to kissing and with so great a skill that she could never have been prepared for it. Even in her most erotic ramblings, she could never have dreamed this. When he pressed her back against the wall, animal instinct consumed her, until there was only one thought in her head, and that was for him to take her. She wanted everything he had to give, the searing kisses, the physical pleasure. The past was obliterated by the searing heat of the present as Khalid teased her lips apart and took possession of her mouth.

With that one kiss he had crossed an invisible line. There was no going back. What had been done could not be undone. But he'd take this slowly. Millie deserved nothing less. She would be properly prepared for pleasure when he took her. Cupping her face in one hand, he mapped the swell of her breasts with the other. They were so full, so firm, he searched for a reaction in her eyes and he wasn't disappointed. She groaned, and covered his hand with hers to urge him on as he lightly abraded the tip of her nipple with his thumbnail before attending to the other breast. Her legs trembled as he moved on to stroke the smooth line of her belly. She sighed rhythmically with approval in time to what he knew would be delicious little twinges of pleasure, and gasped out loud when he captured the swell of her buttocks to press her hard against his straining body. Arching her back, she positioned her bottom high for more touching, but he had decided that that was enough for now.

'Why?' she asked, her voice ringing with disappointment when he stopped.

'Because greedy must learn to wait,' he murmured against her lips.

'I don't want to wait,' she exclaimed.

He could change his mind. An excited breath rushed out of her as he eased her legs apart with his thigh. Having spread her, he allowed his fingertips to trail tantalisingly lower. As he had expected, she gave a sharp cry of need. 'Not yet,' he whispered, teasing her ear lobe with hot breath and his tongue.

'When?' she demanded on a shaking breath as he swung her into his arms.

He carried her deeper into the privacy of his suite, into his bedroom, but as the door closed behind them, enveloping them in opulent silence, he was aware of his body like never before. It felt like a brutal weapon against the yielding accommodation of Millie's soft frame. He had always prided himself on his steely control, but having her here took things to a knife's edge. If Millie had been a different, more experienced woman, his physical hunger was such he would have had her up against the door by now, bringing them both the release they so badly needed.

'I want you,' she whispered urgently against his neck, adding to the torment.

'Temporary relief?' he suggested.

'More than that,' she assured him. 'A lot more,' she added in a voice shaking with excitement. A wild flame of passion burned in her eyes, wiping out reason. It threatened to do the same to him.

'When I decide,' he told her firmly.

'Okay,' she agreed, gulping convulsively. 'Whatever you say.'

She'd agree to anything in her present heightened state. It was up to him to set the pace.

'Please,' she begged, reaching for his belt buckle. Her hands were trembling as she wrenched and tugged until finally the buckle yielded. She gave a little growl like a tiger cub with a thorn in its pad, and then yanked the belt out of its loops. *'Oh!'*

His zipper didn't just slide down, but burst open as he sprang free. Her lips were parted in an expression of such surprise, he wanted to laugh, but that would definitely have broken the mood. Then, she surprised him by exclaiming, 'I can't possibly accommodate *that*.' And now they were both laughing.

'What are you doing to me, Millie Dillinger?' he demanded. This was turning into something far more than a seduction; it was a getting-to-know-you process such as he'd never experienced before, laced with a surprising degree of, *I really like this woman.*

'I mean it,' she said. 'I can't.'

'You might surprise yourself.'

'You'd like to surprise me,' she corrected him. 'Are you a freak, or is this normal?'

'You don't know?' Alarm bells rang loud and clear. Millie was either a virgin, or she was inexperienced beyond any woman he'd ever known. 'This,' he said, 'is normal for me.'

'Hmm.' She considered what he'd said. 'That's

what I thought. And I'm glad you think it's funny,' she added when he laughed out loud.

'Funny?' he queried as he moved away to rearrange his clothing. 'I'm not laughing at you. It's your unique take on things that amuses me.'

'Well, I don't know who you've known before me—'

Her outrage amused him even more, but he curbed the smile in favour of cupping her chin and bringing her close. 'Your expression amuses me, *habibti*. But there is one thing I must ask: are you always this reckless?'

She trembled as he whispered this against her mouth, but he could feel her relief that he'd backed off. 'Never,' she admitted frankly.

Relief, Millie thought as Sheikh Khalid backed off. Narrow escape. And huge disappointment. She couldn't pretend that vigorous, fabulous sex with the best-looking man alive didn't hold enormous appeal, but when he also happened to be her historical enemy, the bogey-man she'd fantasised about pummelling into the ground—when she hadn't been making passionate love to him in her dreams—this shouldn't be happening. And now she had to find a way to exit with dignity.

'There's no need to feel embarrassed,' he said, touching her cheek with tenderness as she awkwardly smoothed her ruffled hair.

'I shouldn't have come back here,' she admitted.

'Yes, you should,' he argued. 'In fact, I'd have been

more surprised if you could stay away when there are so many more questions you want to ask me.'

I can't stay away, Millie silently admitted. While the *Sapphire* was in dock and Khalid was close by, she was always going to be drawn to the disaster, to the fact that her mother died here, and to him, the only person who could tell her more about the events of that night.

'This is part of your history,' he said, gesturing around. 'You shouldn't expect to forget. It wouldn't be natural. You have to learn to handle how you feel about this place.'

'Not if you sail away,' she said. Guilt overwhelmed her as she tried to block out how they'd kissed, how he'd touched her, and how she'd responded to him like an animal on heat, and failed utterly.

Inexperience had let her down, and now Khalid was giving her an out. Perversely, she didn't want that. She wanted to stay with him. She wanted more of his time, and more of his touches. More of him. A spear of jealousy so real she actually gasped with pain pierced her at the thought of all the women he must have known; women who'd felt his hands on their bodies, and who had seen that same desire in his eyes.

'I suppose your score card's off the scale,' she commented spikily on the back of this thought.

His hard face softened into laughter. 'I'm not so bad.' He paused a moment, and then admitted wryly, 'I'm worse.'

'And shameless.' But there was no venom in her comment, only a growing fondness, which was dangerous; she had no doubt the Sheikh was as shrewd in his dealings with women as he was in every other area of his life. 'So, what is your score?' she pressed, bracing herself for the answer.

'Sheikh undefeated,' he said.

CHAPTER SEVEN

MILLIE SAT ALONE in the suite, waiting for Khalid to return from attending to his remaining party guests, her body still thrumming from his expert touch. She shifted uncomfortably on the sofa, before glancing at the time on her phone. It was getting late—surely Khalid had seen everyone he needed to see by now?

She was on the point of going to find Khalid at the party when there was a discreet tap on the door. When she opened it, a young maid called Sadie introduced herself. 'His Majesty's PA sent me to direct you to the Pig and Whistle,' Sadie explained.

For a moment, Millie was confused. 'His Majesty's PA sent you? The Pig and Whistle?' she queried, feeling like a fool as she shook her head.

'The Pig and Whistle is what we call the staff mess,' Sadie explained chirpily in a way that immediately endeared her to Millie. 'It's where we hold our parties, and I'm having one tonight.'

'*Your* party?' Millie queried.

'Well, it's not my party, exactly,' Sadie excused. 'It's a tradition on the *Sapphire* that when His Majesty holds a party the staff that prepared everything for his guests, but who aren't required during the actual event, are allowed to celebrate too. To be honest, we don't need much encouragement,' Sadie confided with a grin. 'It's fantastic working on the *Sapphire*. It's such a great crowd.'

But now Millie was worried. Would Khalid find the time to talk to her? He seemed to be passing her on to somebody else. So was that kiss a real kiss, or a power play? She didn't have enough experience to work it out. And Sadie was waiting for her answer. 'I'd love to come along,' she said honestly. Sadie seemed fun. Being invited to the crew party was a hell of a lot better than hanging around on her own, waiting to see if His Majesty could spare the time to talk to her.

'You'll love it. I promise,' Sadie said as she opened the door. 'There's always loads of good food and fun, and lots of dancing.'

Curious about the next adventure, Millie followed the young maid out of the room.

Where was she? Khalid had expected Millie to seek him out well before the party for his guests had ended, but now the night was drawing to a close and shortly his guests would be leaving. He had checked with his guards, but there was no report of Millie leaving the ship. A bolt of dread had run through him as he alerted his head of security to a potential problem.

It couldn't happen again.

A second tragedy on board the *Sapphire* was unthinkable.

Involving Millie?

'I want every inch of this vessel searched,' he commanded his guards as they lined up in front of him.

'Yes, Your Majesty,' they chanted as one, before separating and spreading out across the ship.

Nothing must happen to her, he determined fiercely as he joined the search.

She'd lost track of time, Millie realised. Her stomach clenched as she glanced at her watch. She hadn't had so much fun for ages. The *Sapphire*'s crew came from all over the world, and there was a strong Irish contingent with music and fun and laughter in their blood. The party in the Pig and Whistle had turned into such a riot she'd been up on the table dancing with Sadie for the past half-hour—

Two things happened in quick succession. One of the men swung Sadie into his arms and carried her away, leaving Millie dancing solo, then everyone else turned to stare at the door.

Oh, no!

As if a bagpipe had deflated, the music died to a tuneless hum. Khalid was standing in the doorway. Tall. Dominating. Stern. He was the dark angel from her past, come to wreak vengeance on a woman who had taken a giant leap over the traces. That would be the same woman with burning cheeks and tangled honey-blonde hair, with her skirt lifted high, and a very silly smile on her face.

A smile that just as quickly died.

'Please carry on,' the Sheikh invited as he ducked

his head to join them in the crew quarters. 'Please,' he said, turning to address the musicians. 'Play on.'

The fiddler, a guitarist, and a banjo player soon started up again, and the drummer plied his beater on the Irish drum, the Bodhrán, and by the time the traditional flute had joined in it was as if there had been no interruption to the party.

'I'm sorry I—'

She got no further before Khalid demanded in an icy tone, 'Why are you still here?'

'We've still to speak— Your PA—'

'My PA was instructed to mention the party in the Pig and Whistle so you could get some food. You didn't have the chance to dine before you left my ship the first time tonight, and I thought you might be hungry. I didn't expect you to stay here all night. You should have found some way to tell me where you were, or have you so easily forgotten the risks on a big ship? I've had guards scouring the *Sapphire* for you.'

Millie bided her time until the door had closed behind them and they were alone in the corridor. 'I haven't forgotten the risks, and I'm sorry if I've put you and your guards to such trouble, but I understood we were to talk further. I waited and waited in your suite for you to return and then Sadie knocked on the door, inviting me to come here, at your behest, I'd imagined. Maybe I was mistaken, but would you have preferred me to have hung around on the deck for hours, waiting for a signal from you that it was convenient for us to talk?'

He stared down at her with no expression on his

face at all, and then he queried softly, 'Dance?' Opening the door to the party, he stood aside to let her pass.

Millie frowned. 'Are you serious?'

'Never more so,' he confirmed. 'Well?'

She was still shell-shocked, both by the sudden appearance of Khalid, and by his offer. She suddenly became acutely aware that her lips were still burning from his earlier kisses, which made the decision to go or stay one hell of a lot more significant than it might have been. 'I'd like that,' she said.

Sheikh Khalid drew her through the throng and, springing up on the table, he lifted her and steadied her in front of him. The noise had reached fever pitch by this time, making it seem that they were in the middle of some primitive rite, with a dark angel and a virgin in the middle of it. And while some men might have looked foolish dancing on a table, as in everything else he did, Khalid was a natural.

Space restriction forced him to keep her pressed hard against his body. 'I won't let you fall,' he promised.

'You'd better not,' she warned.

She felt safe. Even all the history behind them didn't seem to matter. It was hot and steamy in the Pig and Whistle, and the noise was drumming at her head, but it couldn't come between them. They were so closely linked, both physically and mentally, that even here in this crowded space it was as if just the two of them were dancing with no onlookers at all.

'Enough?' he asked when finally she begged for mercy.

'I'm too dizzy to walk,' she protested, staggering as he sprang down from the table.

Reaching up, he brought her safe into his arms.

'Put me down! I feel embarrassed.'

'There's no need,' he said. 'No one's watching. No one cares.'

Everyone cares, Millie thought as the smiling crowd parted to let them through when Sheikh Khalid carried her to the door. It was only natural that they were intrigued. His Majesty and the laundress dancing in the Pig and Whistle? What wasn't cool about that?

When the door closed behind them a second time, Khalid lowered Millie to her feet and stared down at her. 'Are we going to talk?' she asked. 'I guess you need to say goodnight to your guests first, and I'm happy to wait,' she said, thinking it was the least she could do. 'And then I really must get back,' she added to fill the silence when he didn't speak. 'It's getting late.'

'Did you plan to swim back?'

'*What?* I… I'm sorry…?' Millie stared up in utter amazement. 'What do you mean?'

'Just that the *Sapphire*'s been underway for over an hour.'

She couldn't speak. She didn't know what to say. There was nothing *to* say, Millie concluded. She was a stowaway on the Sheikh's yacht? What protection did that give her?

What had she done?

She wracked her brains for a solution, but there was

none. She was stranded at sea with the Sheikh. 'What about your guests?'

'They disembarked some time ago.'

'So, we're heading to…?' She wracked her brains for the closest port to King's Dock on the south coast of England.

'For Khalifa,' he said, as if that were obvious.

'Khalifa?' Millie gasped. 'Halfway around the world?'

She was stunned when he confirmed this. Now she was standing still, she could feel the vibration of the ship's engines beneath her feet and hear the faint hum. 'Couldn't you drop me off somewhere?' she asked, knowing she was clutching at straws.

'This isn't a bus, Ms Dillinger.'

'Of course not, I mean…' For once in her neatly organised life, Millie didn't have a clue what to do next. 'Miss Francine will be worried,' was all she could come up with.

'You can call her,' the Sheikh advised.

It was too late; Miss Francine would be in bed.
Bed.

The single word ricocheted around Millie's head. Where was she going to sleep? The thought of spending the night—maybe many nights—on board the *Sapphire* was unnerving, to say the least.

'You'll feel better when you've had something to eat,' Khalid predicted.

'I doubt that somehow,' she said, but her stomach grumbled on cue.

'You'll eat with me,' he said, leading the way down the corridor.

With little choice, she followed him to the grand salon, where it was hardly possible to imagine that a party had taken place. Everything had been cleared away and calm order restored in the magnificent room.

She stared blankly at the phone as he handed it to her. 'Miss Francine,' he prompted, shaking her out of the trance. 'Make your call and leave a message if she isn't up. While you do that, I'll arrange for refreshments.'

Miss Francine was not only awake, Millie discovered, but both thrilled and amused to hear from her charge. 'Make the most of it,' she said to Millie's amazement.

'But I'm *alone* with him,' Millie exclaimed discreetly with a glance at the Sheikh.

'Wonderful,' Miss Francine enthused. 'A world of women will envy you.'

'What are you saying?' Millie asked in the same hushed tone.

'Just that life is full of choices, and you haven't gone wrong so far, Millie Dillinger.'

'I wish I had your confidence in me,' Millie admitted. 'When I boarded the *Sapphire*, I seemed to leave my common sense on shore.'

'That's your opinion,' Miss Francine said firmly. 'It won't hurt you to unplug for a while, and it might do you a lot of good.'

By the time Millie ended the call, she felt that, if she hadn't exactly been given a licence to maybe break a few boundaries, she did have the confidence of someone she trusted implicitly.

A knock on the door heralded the arrival of stewards bearing platters of delicious-looking food. 'I can't eat all this,' Millie protested as they laid it out on the table.

'Don't worry. I'm here to help,' Khalid assured her.

He took hold of a plate and handed it to her, but when she gripped it he held onto the other side so they were joined by a fragile china bridge. 'I'm not—'

'Hungry?' he suggested. When her cheeks flamed red, he added softly, 'Or do you feel guilty about being a stowaway on my ship?'

'I thought I was your guest?' Should his stern look be sending her pulse off the scale?

'My guests have all left,' he reminded her. 'All except one. Don't look so worried. There's no charge for this cruise.'

And at least they'd get the chance to talk, Millie thought as he urged, 'Eat. You need to keep up your strength.'

For what reason? she wondered. 'Are you sure the *Sapphire* won't be docking at a closer port than Khalifa?' Her badly rattled nerves were clamouring for a solution.

'Enjoy the trip,' Sheikh Khalid recommended as he helped himself to food. 'I'll arrange for a private jet to fly you home when we're done.'

'When we're done?' Millie queried hoarsely. 'I can't just disappear off the grid. I've got a college course to complete.' And a world of ugly memories to move past.

'You're on holiday from college,' the Sheikh observed.

She was no longer surprised by what he knew, only that he cared enough to find out.

'And as I said, I will place a private jet at your disposal. You can leave Khalifa whenever you choose.'

'I'd rather take a commercial flight, thank you.' She had no intention of putting herself in the Sheikh's debt. 'And if you can let me off at a closer port, that would be even better.'

'Your virtue is quite safe with me,' he said.

Was he mocking her? She couldn't really see his eyes. His face was turned away from her.

'You can have the guest suite, and the golden sheets,' he added.

Huzzah, thought Millie, grimacing.

He turned in time to see her expression. 'My friend Tadj has been detained on shore by your friend Lucy.'

This was getting worse and worse. Now she had to worry about Lucy.

Lucy could look after herself, Millie reminded herself. She was facing a more immediate problem. 'I don't even have a change of clothes.'

'You're wrong,' the Sheikh told her. 'Your closet is full.'

'You *planned* this?' she exclaimed with outrage.

Throwing up his hands in mock alarm, he gave a lazy shrug. 'Designers from across the world have rushed to accommodate you.'

'And you expect me to be grateful?' she said. 'I feel as if I've been manipulated all along.'

'Touché, Ms Dillinger. Not much escapes you.'

'You admit it?' Millie exclaimed with incredulity.

The Sheikh didn't bat an eyelid. 'What use is massive wealth if it can't be enjoyed? London is a rich source of luxury goods, and only a short hop by helicopter from King's Dock.'

'I'm going to my room.'

'Please do,' he invited with a gracious gesture towards the door. 'I'm sure you won't be disappointed with what you find there. Just don't forget to come back and tell me what you think. And then we'll talk,' he promised with velvet charm.

Infuriating man! Just as he'd said, the fitted dressing room leading off the gilded stateroom was packed full of Milan's finest clothes, Spain's softest leather shoes, and the best of New York's cutting-edge accessories…

And if that didn't prove to be enough to persuade Millie Dillinger to relax and unwind, Khalid thought as he waited to hear Millie's verdict, he would just have to think of something else. He was no saint, and had never pretended to be. Protecting Millie, versus seducing her, had long since passed its tipping point. She was no longer a child, but a hot-blooded woman, and there was a long ocean voyage ahead of them.

CHAPTER EIGHT

WHEN THE FOOD was cleared away and Millie had returned—acting cool, but still with the glow of pleasing discoveries reflected in her eyes—he persuaded her to walk out on the deck, where a sophisticated heating system ensured she wouldn't be cold this far north, and subdued lighting permitted views of the night sky, as well as a wide swathe of restless sea.

'I'd be happy in the staff quarters,' she assured him as she leaned over the rail...still looking, still searching for the truth, he thought. 'Save the guest suite for someone who appreciates golden sheets,' she said, pulling back as a steward drew out a chair.

'Relax. Enjoy yourself. Sit down,' he encouraged. 'There's nowhere else to go.'

She angled her chin to stare up at him. 'It isn't easy to relax,' she admitted.

'I know,' he said quietly.

She couldn't stop staring at his mouth. She had to stop. But how, when she only had to press her lips together to find they were still swollen from his kisses?

'Don't you want to experience something more exciting than a bunk bed dressed with white cotton for the duration of this trip?' he asked, distracting her.

'If that's your opening gambit, I'm disappointed.' Liar, Millie thought as her pulse careered out of control.

'And I took you for an ambitious woman, Millie Dillinger.'

'I am,' she confirmed, 'but I'll get ahead on my own merit, thank you.'

The Sheikh smiled faintly. 'So no golden sheets?'

He shrugged, and pressed his lips down in a way she found hard to resist.

'I realise I must pay you something for passage on your ship.'

Her prim tone made him laugh. 'I'm sure we'll come to some sort of accommodation.'

'I'm talking about a purely commercial transaction,' she assured him.

'And so am I. What else could I possibly mean?'

Millie firmed her jaw and said nothing.

'And you should know I don't offer credit.'

'This is no joking matter, Your Majesty.'

'I think we've reached a stage where you can safely call me Khalid.'

'Thank you, Your Majesty,' Millie said pointedly. There was nothing safe about any of this. 'If it pleases you—'

'It does please me. Call me Khalid,' he repeated with a slight edge to his voice.

Here was someone who wasn't used to being disobeyed, Millie thought. 'Thank you, *Sheikh* Khalid. I realise the great honour you're doing me, so I will use the polite prefix Sheikh in future.'

This made him groan. 'I'm a man like any other.'

'That's just the point,' she insisted. 'You're not. I'm here because I'm waiting for you to tell me the truth about my mother, and—'

'I'm here because?' he prompted.

'It's a long, cold swim home?' she suggested.

He laughed. It was a wonderful sound. However aloof she tried to be, it seemed Khalid could always cut through her reserve. But what was he thinking now? she wondered as she stared into his brooding face. She could never tell—

She yelped as he cleared the table with a comprehensive sweep of his arm. Everything went flying as he dragged her close and pressed her down onto the cool, hard surface.

'Now what are you going to do?' he asked.

She'd have been angry if it hadn't been for the teasing light in his eyes, because that excited her more than he frightened her. 'Let me go,' she said quietly.

'What if I say no? What are you going to do then?'

'Raise a knee and do you an injury.'

He laughed again. 'And you say that so nicely.'

She held her breath as his wicked mouth tugged into a smile. 'You really are a very bad man,' she observed on a dry throat.

'I really am,' he confirmed, unconcerned.

What a time for her gaze to drop to his mouth!

'Do you want me to kiss you?' he asked.

She drew in a long, shuddering breath. 'It would be nice,' she confessed.

'*Nice?*'

Now he was frowning.

'Very nice?' she suggested.

The tip of Millie's tongue had just crept out to moisten her kiss-bruised lips in a way he found unbearably seductive. Was it deliberate? He concluded, yes. She had the light of mischief in her eyes.

'And when you've kissed me, I still want the truth, and not the edited version you gave me earlier on.'

She said this so coolly he could only admire her nerve. She had a knack of combining business with pleasure in a way he was beginning to doubt he could do when Millie was involved. Cursing viciously in Khalifan, he let her go and straightened up. 'Are you determined to drive me to distraction?'

'That depends on how long it takes,' she said, and, brushing the creases out of her clothes as coolly as you liked, she climbed down from the table.

'You're playing with fire,' he said as she stared into his face.

'I hope so,' she agreed.

Raking a hand through his hair, he began to laugh. 'You win the prize for the coolest and most infuriating woman I've ever met.'

'Good,' she said. 'I'd hate to be an also-ran.'

'As the mistress of the ruling Sheikh of Khalifa, you'd have no competition—'

'Your *mistress*?' Millie repeated as if she had something unpleasant on her tongue. 'Are you telling me, if that were the case, I'd have no competition for your attention?'

'None,' he confirmed.

'Forget it, Your Majesty,' she flared with an incredulous shake of her head. 'Just tell me what I need to know and we're done here.'

'We're done when I say we're done,' he rapped, all out of patience.

'Perhaps you don't think I deserve the truth?' she said, bridling as she confronted him. 'Or maybe you think I can't handle the truth. Either way, you're wrong.'

He'd never had such an outright revolt to handle, and was enjoying the experience. When she started to pick up the mess he'd made when he'd cleared the table, he couldn't just stand and watch.

Khalid, Millie thought. As if she could call the titan currently helping her to clear up the floor Khalid. It was one thing having him inhabit her dreams as a sheikh on horseback, or a hero who took the starring role in every one of her erotic dreams, but calling the real live man Khalid, rather than Your Majesty, or Sheikh Khalid, was way too intimate to even contemplate. If she did that, who knew where it might lead? Not to becoming his mistress, that was for sure, she thought as their arms brushed. Having the Sheikh as her lover might hold huge appeal for her erotic self, because in her dreams she had nothing better to do than enjoy the pleasures of the seraglio, the hidden secrets of the desert, and the sensual pleasures concealed within a Bedouin tent. But in the real world? No chance.

'You wanted to talk,' he reminded her as, job completed, they both stood up again. 'So, let's talk.'

She'd wanted nothing more, but suddenly her mind blanked. 'You don't have to protect my feelings,' she said as the mist cleared. It had occurred to her that maybe he really was trying to protect her. 'I went through all the stages of grief eight years ago.'

'When what happened must have seemed black and white to you,' he said, staring at her keenly.

'Death doesn't come in shades of grey.'

'Indeed not,' Khalid agreed in the same quiet tone.

'My mother was a victim.' She could never say that enough times. It was what she had always believed, totally and utterly. 'The gutter press may have labelled her a pathetic drunk, but she was always a star to me, and she was my mother, and I'll defend her to my last breath. If you know *anything* about that night that could absolve her from any blame or ridicule, I want you to tell me. With the benefit of hindsight, it's easy to see that my mother was deluded, and believed that singing on your brother's yacht might revive her career. It was all she'd got—'

'She had you.'

Yes, *yes*, and the responsibility for leaving the one person who had needed her most alone on this yacht would never leave her. 'Yes, and I left her,' she exclaimed, lashed by guilt. 'Then your brother took advantage of my mother's vulnerability. How can you possibly sanitise that?'

'You still hate me,' he murmured.

'Tell me something to change my mind,' she begged, wishing deep down that there could be proof that Khalid had never been implicated directly. There was no excuse for his brother. The late Sheikh Saif was guilty of murder in Millie's eyes, and all she could do now was to obtain justice for her mother.

'Your mother brought you into danger that night, and that's a fact,' he said as she shook her head slowly and decisively, over and over again. 'My brother's parties were notorious. She must have known.'

'That she was putting me in danger? No. She would never do that.'

'It depends how desperate she was, don't you think?'

'You didn't know her, I did,' she insisted stubbornly.

'She was your mother, and you loved her no matter what. I get that. And I won't go on, if you can't take it.'

'Don't patronise me,' she warned. 'Tell me what you know. You can't stop now.'

He stared at her for a long time before saying anything, as if he had to be sure she wouldn't break down. She nodded once, briskly, inviting him to explain.

Another long pause, and then he said, 'Did you know your mother was a drug addict?'

She battled to suck air into lungs that had inexplicably closed. 'Don't be ridiculous!' she blurted at last. 'Don't you think I'd have known, if that were the case?'

But she did know. At least, she had suspected. And had needed to hear it from someone else, someone who was deeply involved. Miss Francine had always protected Millie from the truth, and she loved her for it. Khalid had done her another type of kindness by not dressing up the truth, and perhaps his was the greater gift, because he'd given her closure at last.

'How did you know?' she asked, feeling the tension seep away as the last piece of the jigsaw settled into place. Her fury at Khalid had been instantly replaced by deep sorrow for her mother.

Taking hold of her hands, he brought them down from her face. 'I'm sorry,' he said quietly. 'I think everyone must have known about your mother's habit apart from you.'

'I think I knew,' she whispered. 'I'd read rumours in the press, but I didn't want to believe them. She was always careful around me, so I never saw any proof. Thank you for telling me. I needed to hear it. Then...' She braced herself to voice the unspeakable. 'If my mother was the freak show, was I the support act? Did your brother ever speak to you of that?'

His intention was not to destroy Millie, but to try and lay her ghosts to rest. His late brother would accept no restraint on his perversions. Whatever Millie asked of him now, he had to edit the truth, or cause her endless pain. 'I didn't know there was a party on board the *Sapphire* that night, until I arrived,' he explained. 'And as for your mother taking drugs? She would hardly be

the first great artist to fall foul of ruthless and unscru-
pulous drug dealers.'

'But that doesn't explain her death,' Millie said,
frowning.

He wasn't about to explain that he'd chased her
mother's drug dealer into the arms of the police, and
had been dockside when Roxy's body was fished out of
the harbour. He'd checked to see if there was a pulse,
and had seen the sapphires spilling over the top of her
dress. He'd retrieved them before he was asked to stand
back, so at least she could never be branded a thief.

'Did she fall or was she pushed?'

Millie's voice was hoarse, and her face was pale
and strained. She deserved an honest answer, and at
least he could give her this. 'The dealer pushed her
into the water.'

Over her gasp, he told her the rest of it—or his interpretation of what must have happened on that terrible night. He guessed Roxy had tried to pay the man
for her fix in sapphires, which the dealer would assume were fake. Khalid guessed that was when he lost
his temper. He'd seen little more than the end of the
fight. The *Sapphire* was a huge vessel, so by the time
he reached the shore, calling the authorities as he ran,
he was too late to save Millie's mother.

'You saw this happen,' she stated tensely, 'so you
were watching her all along.'

'I witnessed something,' he said honestly. 'I was
too far away to see clearly, and when I arrived at the
scene it was dark and the water was black.'

'But you called the authorities, so you must have known something was badly wrong.'

'I heard a scream. That was what attracted my attention. It could have been kids acting up. It was only a few seconds later when I realised it wasn't a game, and by then it was too late.'

'I asked you to go back to save her,' Millie said quietly. All her frustration and grief collided. 'You bastard!' she exclaimed, launching herself at him. 'You let her down. And I know there's something you're not telling me. I know it—*I know it*!'

Catching hold of her, he held her still. 'It's over, Millie. It's over now.'

As she fought him and railed against him, he wished he could do more, say more, but with a bride looming in his very near future he would not make any false promises to Millie. He could only wait until her anger burned out, and when it did, and she slumped against him, completely spent, he let her sob.

He waited until she was quiet again, and then tipped up her chin. 'Where are you taking me?' she asked as he took hold of her hand.

'To bed—'

'Are you mad?' she exclaimed. 'Let go of me!'

Ignoring her request, Khalid steered her on through the ship. The elevator was closer than the companionway and he stopped in front of it. Within seconds he'd backed her into the small, plush space. It did no good raging. He stood in her way, blocking her only escape route as the doors slid slowly to.

'My intention is not to make you forget the past,'

he said quietly as she stood stiff as a board, pressed up hard against the corner, 'but to help you face the facts and deal with them.'

'How very kind,' she said tensely. Her emotions were shot. She should have realised what a trauma it would be coming back. If she'd stayed on board eight years ago and shadowed her mother, this wouldn't be happening, and her mother would still be alive.

'No,' Khalid instructed in a low tone as she covered her face with her hands. 'No,' he repeated. 'This is not your fault.'

This was all her fault. Snapping around so she didn't have to look at him, she slammed her forearm against the padded wall and buried her face in her arm. But reality had a way of intruding. What chance would she have stood against the toad-like Sheikh Saif and his guards?

Maybe none, but she should have tried.

'No,' Khalid said again, this time in a sharper tone when she reached for the controls to try and open the doors of the elevator before it moved off. 'It's too late for that.'

Too late for everything, she thought as he kept her boxed in the corner as the car began to rise. When she tried to push him away, he caught hold of her wrists and pinned them above her head. Frustration grabbed her by the throat. The need to learn secrets he refused to tell her exploded in fury and she snarled like a wild animal caught in a trap. He had an answer for that too. Dipping his head, Khalid enforced silence with a kiss.

And not just any kiss, but one that melted her from the inside out. She only had to taste him, feel him, scent him, touch him, and she was lost. He was everything missing from her life. His touch seared her senses. His kisses rocked her world. Being lost in his arms always blotted out the past. He offered oblivion, and that was exactly what she craved right now. If she thought any more about the past, she'd go mad.

The elevator slowed to a halt, but he sent it down again. He pressed another light on the panel and it stopped between floors. 'What are you doing?' she asked tensely.

'Taming you,' he said, shocking her to her core. 'Helping you to forget...'

What did that mean? Her wrists were still captive in his one massive fist, and with his free hand he began to map her breasts. Stunned, excited, angry, eager; she was all of those things. Her knees actually shook when he kissed her this time. Her body felt as if it had been plugged into a power source. She gasped when he grazed her nipples with his thumbnail. And vocalised her need for more when he weighed her breasts appreciatively before stroking them with the most seductive touch. She was incapable of speech, not that it mattered. Khalid was so intuitive he didn't need any instruction, and telling him to stop was the last thing she wanted to do. Pulses of pleasure streamed straight to her core, leaving her with only one possible destination.

'Need is blazing in your eyes,' he observed, sounding pleased. 'But if you'd like me to stop—'

Her excited laugh gave him the only answer he needed. She was a willing prisoner in Khalid's erotic net, and her reward was the brush of his sharp black stubble against her neck, and then the lightest brush of his lips as he kissed her. When he took possession of her mouth with his tongue, she found it too arousing, too tempting, and as he deepened the kiss she rubbed against him. She needed that big, hard body pressing into hers. Desperate for more contact, she writhed shamelessly against him. He tasted of everything good, and she was putty in his hands. Animal sounds of pleasure escaped her throat as his hand slid slowly up her leg.

Done with begging, she commanded, 'I need you.'

'Open your legs. Wider,' he instructed.

He had never felt such an urge to pleasure a woman. Thrusting his thigh between hers, he spread her wide. Her excited cries greeted his first touch. The change in her was instantaneous. From being her avowed enemy, he was her lifeblood and she would do anything he asked. Sinking onto his palm, she ground her body against the heel of his hand.

'Not so fast,' he cautioned.

Releasing her wrists, he held her securely in place while he traced the hot swell of her sex. Removing her thong, he found the tip that craved his attention and circled it. Teasing Millie was torture for him, but it was also its own reward, and with so many days at sea ahead of them, he could afford to take his time.

'Please!' Millie begged in a voice that was trembling with need. Clinging to him, she worked her hips in a desperate hunt for more contact.

'Do you expect me to obey you?' he asked with amusement.

'You can't leave me like this.'

'Can't I?'

'Please don't.'

He smiled against her mouth as she threatened to make him pay for his cruel neglect.

'I'm counting on it,' he said as he began the slow and deliberate circling as she frantically worked her hips.

'Don't tease me,' she begged in a strangled tone as she tried every which way to bring her body into contact with his hand.

Adjusting the position of his fingertip by millimetres was all it took for him to change the outcome. Increasing both pressure and speed by the smallest degree quickly brought Millie the release she so desperately needed. Her screams of relief were deafening and prolonged. She had waited a long time, he guessed, and would need a lot more before she was sated.

Holding her safe in his arms until she quietened, he kissed her and then murmured, 'Bed?'

'Just more of that,' she said, resting against him as she dragged in air. 'Wherever—'

Sending the car up to his deck, he lifted her into his arms and carried her to his suite.

CHAPTER NINE

HAVING LAID HER down on his bed, Khalid kicked off his shoes. Millie's cheeks were burning as incredulity and excitement washed over her in turn, at what she'd done, and what she was about to do. All thoughts of leaving the *Sapphire* as soon as possible and flying home, forgetting any of this had ever happened, had vanished as surely as mist before the sun. Khalid had freed her. He'd seen her lose control completely and, having given him that, there was no reason now to hold back.

She turned to look around as his clothes hit the floor and felt the blood drain from her cheeks. What was she thinking? He was massive and tanned, hard muscles sculpted like a Michelangelo statue; there was so much of beautiful, perfect him, and all of it in formidable proportion.

'Shy now?' he asked with amusement.

'No,' she defended, but he heard the lie in her voice.

Coming to join her on the bed, Khalid stretched out his magnificent, naked length alongside her and, resting his chin on the heel of his hand, he viewed her steadily as if she were a new and fascinating exhibit on board his yacht. He knew how aroused that made her, and how aroused she still was after his skilful attention. 'You want me,' he said.

The faint smile on his mouth was all it took to make her want him even more. 'Not as much as you want me,' she countered, determined, even at this late stage, to fight her corner.

He shrugged and his lips pressed in response.

'If you didn't want me, why are we here?' she asked with perfect logic, she thought. 'Unless you invite all your female guests to share your bed?'

This made him laugh. 'Millie, Millie, Millie. Do you think I make a habit of stopping my elevator between decks?'

'I don't know. I'd rather not think about it,' she admitted. 'I'm sure there are those who think there are advantages to be gained by sleeping with you, but I'm not one of them.'

'No,' he whispered, 'You're not.'

He'd been toying with a lock of her hair as she spoke, and now he drew her into his arms. A great hunger swept over him for more than sex: to be joined, to be close, to give pleasure. This would be a sensuous and lengthy seduction. Millie was young and inexperienced, and deserved nothing less. The reward would be extreme pleasure. The thought of sinking into her hot, eager body was—

'Where are you going?' she asked as he moved away. Reaching for his hand, she caught hold of his wrist. Her boldness made him smile. She was a tigress.

'I'm twice your size.'

'Good,' she said, her grip firming. Her gaze was steady on his face.

Physical pleasure was a gift, to be cherished and worked on. It was not enough to become a great warrior, he had been told by the elders of the desert; a man must prove himself a great lover too. Eroticism was valued by the travelling tribes he'd joined as a youth, when he'd had no expectation of becoming the ruling sheikh of Khalifa.

'Your Majesty seems distracted.'

'By you,' he said, staring down into Millie's laughing eyes. 'You distract me.' He toyed thoughtfully with a strand of her long, silky hair. 'I'll keep you safe.'

'I don't want to be safe,' she whispered fiercely.

'What do you want?'

'To forget,' she said as she closed her eyes.

Coming back to lie close, he soothed her trembling body with long, rhythmical strokes. The bond between them was tightening. Was that fair to Millie?

Being naked in bed with Khalid was a recipe for skewing her thoughts. Drugging and amazing, it was as if every nerve ending she had were standing to attention. Moving her body with increased confidence against his heightened her senses as never before. The lights were out and night enfolded them in a thick black velvet blanket. His soothing strokes and the almost imperceptible movement of the big ship added to her arousal. Cupping her face in his hands, he kissed her in a way that made tears spring to her eyes. She was glad of the dark, shielding her. Her emotions were raw. She forgot her concern as he mapped her body with knowing skill. 'How long does the teasing go on?' she asked, aching with need.

'As long as I deem it necessary——'

She gasped as he swung her on top of him. There was no avoiding the thrust of his arousal, and no way to call this safe. She was equally intimidated by his size, and excited by it. Her body quivered with expectation, though she wasn't even sure she could take him. On the edge, hovering dangerously close to plunging over, she thought, Spread me wide and take me. Make me forget.

'Will you teach me all you know?' she asked. 'Stop it,' she warned when she saw his teasing expression. How could she not want this man? Outwardly stern, privately human—even warm, she thought. He might be twice her size, but the time for caution was over. Winding her legs around his, she proved her trust. He brought them even closer to kiss her lips, her neck, and then her breasts, as he continued to tease her with feather touches. Moving down the bed, he treated her breasts to a feast of pleasure, and with each insistent tug, she experienced a corresponding pulse between her legs.

'Is this what you want?' he asked, raising his head. He smiled faintly, teasing her again with delay.

'As if you don't know,' she whispered.

Running his fingertips over her breasts, he moved on to stroke her belly, which was incredibly arousing. 'And this?' he asked as he parted her legs.

'So much,' she gasped out.

Lifting her buttocks, he rested them on a soft pillow to spread her wide, and then he arranged her legs comfortably over the powerful width of his shoulders. She almost lost control at the first touch of his tongue. She'd never experienced anything like this. Sensing how close she was, he pulled back, his expression stern.

'When I say you can and not before,' he warned. 'The delay is for your benefit,' he added.

She didn't doubt it as eager forerunners of that bigger release gripped her repeatedly. She had everything to learn, and was a most willing pupil. But nothing—*nothing* could have prepared her for this. Khalid knew exactly how to prolong her pleasure, and when to hold back, until she felt as if every delicious pulse of sensation she had ever experienced had gathered and was waiting to be unleashed.

'Now, please,' she begged.

This resulted in a little more attention on his part, but not enough to tip her over the edge.

Resting back, she closed her eyes, temporarily defeated. When she opened them again, the expression in Khalid's eyes was enough to send her over, but he was the master of pleasure, and knew how to keep her under control.

Short, sharp, noisy gasps shot from her throat as he returned to teasing her with his tongue. She gripped the bed, fists turning white. How much longer was she supposed to hold on? She loved his hands on her buttocks, so firm, so sure as he lifted her to his mouth. A fierce desire to isolate the place where sensation ruled consumed her. Reaching down, she helped him by pressing her legs apart even more, and now she was floating, suspended on a plateau of sensation, where there was no possibility of rational thought and only one way down.

'Now.'

He spoke the single word so softly. It was the only prompt she needed. 'Now!' she agreed fiercely.

Her body worked with wild abandon to capture the waves of pleasure as Khalid buffeted her rhythmically. He was amazing, launching her into a world of pleasure that beat at her senses; he showed no mercy when she wailed, and made sure she experienced every last throb of ecstasy until she fell back, utterly exhausted and yet hungry for more.

'You are so aroused,' he remarked, staring down. 'So warm and plump and pink, and accommodating. Good,' he approved, holding her firmly in place when she surprised herself with a second release that didn't require his involvement. He had unlocked something in her that demanded to be fed. 'Hold yourself wide,' he instructed.

She was eager to do so. It was a sign of how far she'd come. All she wanted was this, and Khalid deep inside her, pressing her down into the bed. She could think of nothing else.

Protecting them both, he teased her with his body. She wailed with disappointment when he pulled away, and was instantly hungry for more.

'Yes?' he asked, giving her a little more.

Grabbing hold of him, she worked her hips as he

circled her core with the same teasing skill, before entering her again, just an inch or so. 'No!' she complained angrily when he withdrew.

'We take this slowly,' he explained in a husky whisper.

She didn't want 'slowly'. She wanted firm and fast and hard. And deep...so deep. 'Please,' she begged, writhing provocatively beneath him.

Pinning her wrists above her head, he teased her repeatedly, each time sinking a little deeper. 'Yes,' she groaned as he took her by thrilling degrees, 'Oh, yes...'

When he was lodged to the hilt, he worked his hips round and round and from side to side, making it impossible not to claim a greedy release.

'That was naughty,' he scolded when she quietened. 'Did I say you could?'

'You didn't say I couldn't,' Millie countered. 'And it's your turn now.'

'Not for a long time yet,' he said, starting up a rhythmical pattern that made further argument the last thing in her head.

She didn't wait, and as she greedily flew into pleasure, he remarked, 'You *are* on a knife's edge,' making it sound like the best sort of praise.

You have no idea, Millie thought as she bucked back and forth to claim the very last pulse of pleasure. She'd had no idea she was even capable of such extremes, or that this would fast become as necessary as breathing to her. 'I'll never get enough of you,' she admitted, her voice muffled against Khalid's chest.

'I look forward to putting that to the test,' he said.

Raising her face to his, he kissed her with such lingering intensity that this time she couldn't hide her tears.

What the hell was he thinking? Khalid mused as he paced the deck outside his stateroom. Dawn was breaking. Millie was still sleeping, so at least he had a chance to think. Was he going to trample her feelings a second time? Crumpling the note handed to him by his aide de camp, he cursed viciously. In the shower before he'd received the note, he had pictured taking her to the desert, but now everything had changed. A rumble of thunder drew his attention to the sky where storm clouds were gathering. The change in the weather was a reminder that nothing remained the same. A prospective bride had arrived uninvited in Khalifa, and was waiting with her family in the guest wing of his palace in the capital. It was politically expedient to meet her, for her brother was one of the Sapphire Sheikhs.

However many times he tried to tell himself this voyage was an entertaining interlude and nothing more, Millie's trusting face appeared in front of him. A slave to duty, who was determined to give his people better after Saif had almost ruined Khalifa with his excesses, Khalid owed it to his people to marry and provide them with an heir. He was expected to make a political alliance, a business transaction between neighbouring countries to strengthen borders and improve trade. His personal wishes didn't come into it.

Then change tradition.

He laughed out loud as the thought occurred to him.

It was so simple in theory, and yet impossible. Things moved too slowly; they always had.

Then change them.

He placed the call.

'I will be in the desert for the next month,' he informed one of his aides at the palace. 'Please give my apologies to the Princess and her family. I will endeavour to make up for this confusion with a substantial donation to their wildlife protection scheme.'

He felt a surge of triumph when he cut the line, then wondered if a month in the desert with Millie would be too long. She commanded his attention like no one else. Maybe a month wouldn't be long enough! When she came out on deck to join him, swathed in a cashmere throw because the *Sapphire* was still heading for warmer climes, he knew he'd made the right decision. Bathed in the clear, early light of dawn, she looked so young and innocent, and yet her cheeks were flushed with a new understanding of pleasure.

'I missed you,' she whispered, clinging to him, and when she raised her face, her eyes were bright with love.

'Did you sleep well?' he asked.

'What do you think?' Millie murmured, and instead of looking behind them, to where there was no longer any British shore to see, she stared ahead with him, to the future and to Khalifa.

They kissed and he wound his hands through her soft bright hair. It fell in lustrous waves to her waist, though it was a little tangled, and he loved that, because it reminded him of the pleasure they'd shared. Linking fingers, he kissed her again, and when finally they broke apart his decision had been made. 'Be ready in half an hour,' he told her.

'Ready for what?' she asked.

'For the adventure to continue.' When she looked at him for more information, he added, 'We'll travel by helicopter first, and then on by private jet to Khalifa.'

'Khalifa,' she breathed. Worry and anticipation battled for supremacy in her eyes.

'Don't change your mind now,' he warned good-humouredly. 'I know you're as impatient as I am to see my homeland.'

'I'm curious,' she agreed, biting her lip as she admitted this.

'More than that, I think. Pack a small case with essentials.' When she started to question him, he said, 'You'll only need a small bag. You'll find one in your dressing room. Everything else will be waiting for you at our destination.'

'Khalifa,' she repeated, still a little wary, but unable to hide her growing excitement.

'Now, be quick,' he urged as he kissed her.

Millie's first sight of the desert knocked the breath from her lungs. Whatever she'd been expecting, this was more. After swooping low over a bright blue sea, they had landed on a small, private airstrip close to the beach where a large marquee had been erected, and uniformed attendants stood in an orderly row, waiting to greet them. The men were dressed in black, their faces covered apart from their eyes. Dressed in tunics and baggy trousers, with long, curving daggers secured inside their belts, they were an intimidating sight. A sense of unreality struck her as she looked around, trying to take everything in. With a backdrop of burnished blue sky, blazing sun and endless sand, the scene was like something out of a thrilling and exotic movie. And she was playing one of the leading roles with a man at her side who made every film star seem like a pallid sham. This was real, and this was incredible.

A red carpet led from the steps of the jet to the enormous white tent, on top of which fluttered Khalid's personal insignia: the hawk of the desert in black and gold on a red ground. Having piloted the helicopter from the superyacht, Khalid had flown them in one of his private jets from the large international airport. There was no sign of a limousine or sleek SUV waiting to take them on to their next destination. Instead, a number of horses were tethered beneath the shade of a large awning...

'Welcome to Khalifa,' Khalid said, distracting her from the lavishly caparisoned horses as he urged her forward.

Everything was very new and very strange and very wonderful. His hand on her arm was reassuring. And arousing. The look in his eyes was hypnotising. After so many hours of enforced separation in the jet, she longed for his prolonged attention—time alone, to confide and make love. His steadying hand was both a curb on those thoughts, and a reminder of the pleasure they'd shared.

'What do you think?' he said as he turned to look at her at the entrance to the grand pavilion.

'Amazing.' She stared past the guards to the rich colours in the womb-like, shadowy interior. 'It's certainly a contrast to home.' Where a subdued colour palette ruled at King's Dock thanks to the regular rainfall.

'Millie?'

Having no experience of the desert, other than in books, she was overcome by the vastness of the sand stretching away on every side for unseen miles. She was nothing more than a grain of sand in the grand scheme of things. 'I'm disorientated,' she confessed. 'I've never seen anything on this scale.' And she was a long way from home.

This journey was reckless. She was miles away from anything familiar, with only a mobile phone and a failing battery between her and complete isolation. She must place her trust in Khalid. And her own, keenly developed sense of survival, Millie reminded herself as she followed him into the shade.

'You'll be cooler in here.'

He was right. With no obvious sign of air-con, the billowing tent was cool and airy inside.

'Well?' he asked as she stared around.

'It's wonderful. I can't believe I'm here,' she exclaimed as she walked across the rugs to admire some ancient wall hangings. 'It's such a soothing setting.' The stench of aviation fuel had been shut out, and was replaced by the evocative scent of spice. 'I love it,' she said, turning back to face Khalid. This was no Hollywood replica of a warrior king's tent, but a shaded sanctuary, illuminated by the glow of golden lanterns. Fabrics in a rich variety of jewel shades made it welcoming, while bowls of freshly picked fruit, and jugs of juice waited on a pierced golden table to tempt them. 'All this for us,' she said. 'For you, anyway,' she amended with a wry smile.

'This is for your pleasure,' he argued softly.

'Well, it's fabulous. It's a travelling palace.'

'That's exactly what it is.'

'Lucky man,' she murmured.

As Khalid gave a rueful and accepting shrug, she knew in her gut she'd be okay. There was no need to be overawed by any of this. This was as much his reality as her bedsit in King's Dock was hers. Everything she'd seen so far spoke of care, and appreciation for the craftsmanship and the materials of his country. Photographs of Bedouin tents did them no justice at all.

'You must change into robes before we leave,' Khalid said, distracting Millie from examining the many beautiful examples of art from his homeland.

'You don't expect me to ride, do you?' she exclaimed, remembering the horses. 'I'm not a horsewoman.'

'You might surprise yourself,' he said. 'I'm going to change. I suggest you do too.' He indicated another area of the tent. 'You'll find some clothes in there. I'll help you with the headdress. It takes some getting used to,' he explained as she went to investigate.

Millie's eyes widened at the sight of a beautiful silver-grey robe in the finest of fabrics laid out on a leather daybed. Delicate silver embroidery around the neck and hem, ornamented with tiny seed pearls, had obviously been painstakingly hand-stitched.

'Ready?' Khalid called out while she was still running her fingertips reverently over the intricate work.

'Yes,' she lied.

When he thrust the cover aside it was too late to take those words back. When he strode in, her voice deserted her, anyway. Having changed out of the jeans and shirt he had worn for piloting the plane, Khalid was once again dressed in robes. A true master of the desert, he was a stunning sight. Picking up the glorious grey robe she was to wear, he maintained eye contact as he dropped it over her head. 'It suits you,' he remarked. 'Now take all your other clothes off.'

'Everything?' Millie blinked.

'This is the desert, not the high street, and you're not about to catch a bus.'

She frowned. 'Okay—' But before she could do as he instructed, Khalid had reached down to lift the hem of her robe. Deftly removing her top and jeans, he indicated that she should step out of them. Her underwear followed, leaving her naked beneath the flowing robe.

'What are you doing?' she asked as he lifted her. For a moment she thought there was some other garment he was about to help her to put on.

'Being an extremely bad man,' he said.

She laughed with excitement as his beard-roughened jaw raked her neck.

'No one will disturb us here,' he explained, 'and I'm not going to waste time teasing you, or preparing you.'

'No need.'

But he did test her for readiness. Always so caring. And he protected them both. She had to muffle her cries of pleasure against his chest as he took her in one firm thrust. Needing no encouragement to work furiously with him, she ground her buttocks against his big rough hands. They were both noisy and fierce, both craved fast release. She wrapped her legs tightly around his waist, while her hands gripped his shoulders as if she would never let him go.

'Yes!' she cried as he upped the tempo and force of his thrust. 'I need this—need you! *Ah...!*'

'As I need you, *habibti*!' Khalid ground out, working dependably, rhythmically, firmly.

'Oh...!' Her cries went on and on, as sensation exploded between them in the same instant. How could anything be this amazing, and fantastic and essential to life?

'Again,' Khalid suggested against her ear, in a seductive, warm and teasing tone when the first storm had passed and she had begun to quieten.

'Oh, yes, please,' she agreed.

Settling deep, she gasped, 'Need more...need more...'

Incredibly, with his own release only moments behind him, Khalid was still fully aroused, and as hungry as she was. He thrust firmly and deep, moving persuasively as his big hands helped her to thrust her hips in time with his. 'Must be your turn again?' she gasped after he had satisfied her several times more.

'Like this?' he said, starting over.

'Exactly like that,' she confirmed, howling with pleasure as he upped the pace.

It was a long time later, when they had both taken a shower *and* each other *in* the shower, in a bathroom in the pavilion that surprised Millie by being extremely well equipped, that Khalid towelled her dry, and when that was done he stood before her completely naked.

'Not this time,' he scolded when she reached for him. 'But soon,' he promised.

That had to be enough for her. For now. The desert suits him, she thought as Khalid dropped the black robe over his head. Securing a different type of head-dress from the usual—she knew this was called a *howli*, and called for yards of fabric to be expertly wound around his head and face—he was instantly transformed from a passionate lover, into passionate lover who was also an imposing desert king.

'You can't be cold,' he remarked as she shivered with unadulterated lust.

Khalid's physicality was staggering. Having thought herself sated, she wanted him again, and with a hunger that threatened to overwhelm her.

Even though she could only see his eyes, they were knowing, and quite capable of delivering a message through the narrow slit he had left for his eyes, and that message said, no chance. 'I'll help you put your headdress on,' he said as he gathered up her scarf. 'It will protect you from the sun, and from the sand.'

Alone with her thoughts as he did this, she questioned her feelings and her behaviour. She was having the most wonderful adventure, but what then? However wonderful this was, he was, there was no future for them. Khalid was the powerful ruler of a fabulously wealthy country. She was a laundress from the docks. He couldn't hold off his marriage for ever, and that would have to be a formal and very public affair, and where would that leave Millie? This wasn't going anywhere except back to Khalid's bed, she accepted as she followed him outside; a thought that excited her far more than it should have done.

'You'll ride with me,' he said. 'If you're as inexperienced on horseback as you used to be in bed, it's the safest way to travel,' he murmured discreetly, though she wasn't sure his guards weren't actually mannequins dressed for the role, as they maintained their distance and their silence, and their stillness, admirably. 'As you have discovered,' Khalid added with a wicked smile, 'neither condition needs to remain permanent. Now come closer so I can put the final touches to your head covering to protect you from the sun.'

She had pulled it back a little, and now asked, 'Is it safe?'

'I've never known scarves to bite.'

'I mean you. Are *you* safe?' she scolded. 'Coming close to you, I mean.'

'It's never stopped you before.'

Her body thrilled with memories as he rearranged her headdress, and then led her towards the horses. And the desert.

CHAPTER TEN

'THERE,' KHALID SAID, standing back to examine his handiwork. 'Apart from your striking blue eyes, you look like a real Khalifan.'

She felt unrecognisable: exotic, unusual, and so unlike her usual self.

'Well?' he prompted. 'What do you think?'

'It feels wonderful,' she admitted. 'Cool and comfortable.'

'I sense a but?' he queried.

Only that same niggle of doubt that had struck her inside the tent. What was she doing here, living a dream that didn't belong to her? And never could?

Miss Francine's voice came into her head. *If things appear too good to be true, they generally are.*

She had to shake that thought away, and enjoy each new experience to the full otherwise her time here was wasted. There were never any guarantees in life, so why not make the most of this? She was under the protection of the hawk of the desert. What could possibly go wrong? Millie thought as Khalid's attendants brought up the horses. The air was warm and scented with the tang of the ocean, and adventure in the desert beckoned.

'I'm ready,' she confirmed.

Khalid's snorting, frothing, fearsome-looking animal was definitely not her mount of choice. 'You don't seriously expect me to ride on that?' she said as he beckoned to her to come closer, so he could lift her onto the saddle in front of him. 'That isn't a horse, it's a muscle machine with evil intentions.'

'Play nice, Burkan,' he said as the horse flattened its ears.

'What about me?' Millie pointed out. 'I'm prepared for nice, but preferably when it arrives on four wheels.'

'You'll be fine,' Khalid assured her as he held out his hand.

Black as night, and as hard-muscled as his master, his stallion was grandly caparisoned in red and gold as befitted the favourite mount of a mighty ruler. And had the temperament of a snake someone had poked with a stick, Millie concluded. 'He's a monster. No way. Don't you have a mule, or a donkey?'

'*Burkan* means volcano in your language,' the monster's master explained fondly as he caressed his mount's suddenly pricked-up ears.

'I see he responds to flattery like most males,' Millie commented dryly.

Khalid laughed, the sound muffled behind the *howli*, making it sound like a deep rumble of thunder, while his big black stallion raked the ground and gave her the dead eye. 'He's a pussycat,' he soothed.

'Of the big cat variety, with a thorn in its paw,' Millie agreed.

'I'm right out of donkeys,' Khalid told her, 'so are you coming, or not?'

She gazed around at the desert. This might be his home, but it looked like hostile territory to Millie. Resistant though she was to the idea of riding half a ton of power-packed, mean-eyed horse, she took hold of Khalid's hand. No stallion with a personality disorder was going to frighten Millie Dillinger.

The next moment they were off. There was no slow build up to a flat-out gallop, so she could get used to the stallion's gait. Burkan only knew one speed, and that was rocket-propelled. She yelped with fear as he galloped on, and for a few moments she was sure she'd fall off, but as Khalid's arms tightened around her, her confidence grew.

'Good?' he demanded as Burkan's hooves ate up the desert at a pace she could hardly believe.

'I'm alive,' she yelled back. And that was enough. But soon she realised it was fabulous. There could be nothing better than this wild ride through the desert in the arms of a desert king.

Dunes rose on either side of them, and Millie had no idea how anyone could navigate their way around when everything looked so similar. Khalid had no difficulty. He spearheaded the troop of men. Seeing the land he loved like this told her more about a complex man than hours of conversation ever could. Khalid might be hugely civilised on the outside, but in his heart, he was a fierce desert warrior.

* * *

Seeing his land through Millie's eyes was a wonderful experience, like seeing the desert for the first time. Slowing Burkan, he pointed out the signs he looked for in a landscape, that at first sight appeared confusingly similar, and had the added complication of changing day by day as wind shifted both the shape and position of the dunes. He reined in at the top of one of these sand mountains to give Millie a chance to appreciate the extent of the sea of gold surrounding them. Dismounting, he lifted her down. Kneeling, he showed her the animal tracks in the seemingly sterile environment. He could tell she was fascinated as she knelt down beside him, and they were soon fully engrossed in discussing his plans to turn part of the desert into a fruitful garden, and how he intended to expand his nature reserves in order to protect the most endangered species. When he looked at her to weigh her reaction, and saw how intently she was listening, he felt a swell of emotion akin to love. This was dangerous, he thought as he sprang to his feet.

'Khalifa is *so* beautiful,' she said, standing by his side. 'You're a very lucky man.'

'Yes, I am,' he agreed, striding away to remount Burkan before he said something to make things worse. His growing feelings for Millie were not only inappropriate, but unfair to her. His future was fixed. If not this latest contender who had arrived unannounced at the palace, he must find an appropriate bride soon. It was his duty to settle down and have children, to forge the stable dynasty his people longed for. He could offer Millie nothing in the long-term. He had to content them both with this short desert adventure.

'Come,' he said, reaching down from the saddle. 'We have some miles to cover before we reach the oasis.'

'The oasis?' she exclaimed. 'How romantic.' She stared up with eyes full of wonder, like a child at Christmas, making his decision to follow duty even harder.

'It's where we'll sleep,' he said crisply, trying not to think about the moment of parting, which must come soon, when they would both return to stark reality.

She felt better this time, on the horse, more relaxed, and at one with Khalid. She was excited as they cantered on through the desert towards the promise of a cooling oasis. Having seen this other side of her desert lord, a side that was tender and caring, and deeply committed to the welfare of his country, she loved him more than ever. Yes. Love. There was no other way to describe her growing feelings for Khalid. She didn't want to leave him, or his country, and she was hungry to know more, about him, about Khalifa. Everything that mattered to him mattered to her.

'Isn't it beautiful?' he asked as they rode on through golden dunes with chocolate shadows.

'It's fabulous,' she said as a hawk soared overhead, calling piercingly to its mate.

Everything she'd seen so far was fabulous in Khalifa. The sun, as it dropped lower in the metallic blue sky, was fabulous. The warm scented air was fabulous.

This experience of riding a horse that she'd been so scared of and now loved and appreciated was fabulous. Khalid loved Khalifa and she loved him.

So much, so dangerous, Millie thought. Where did she imagine this was leading? She wasn't stupid. She'd be going home soon. Her dreams of becoming a marine engineer had been put on hold, but she'd pick them up when she went home, while Khalid's destiny kept him here, wrapped up in a life of duty, which he would never renounce.

He would need a wife to sit beside him on the Sapphire throne.

She actually shuddered at the thought, and couldn't bring herself to picture the woman who would support him in everything he did; give him children, live with him and love him. His marriage was sure to be reported in the press, and she would have to be happy for him. It wouldn't be easy, but was the price she had to pay for this...

She stiffened with misery, and that was enough to alert Khalid to a problem. 'Are you all right?' he asked. 'There isn't far to go now.'

She'd gone far too far already, Millie thought. How would this highly charged expedition end? In tears? Or triumph? In understanding? Or in the same fog in which she had instigated their meeting when the *Sapphire* returned to King's Dock? She had never been happier than she was now. Wasn't that enough? Some people didn't have this much. Was she being greedy? Weren't a few days of true happiness better than none?

Khalid had slowed the pace of his stallion, and his

arms were gentle as she rested back against his chest. Did he feel the same need she did to stretch every second remaining to them into an hour, a day, until there were no days left?

Perhaps sensing that her thoughts were racing on into the future, he reined in at the top of a dune, and asked, 'Why don't you tell me about your ambitions?'

Millie was speechless as she looked at the view. Miles of rolling sand dunes, with what appeared to be a lush, green park right in the middle of them. And in the centre of that, there was a glittering oasis, like a wide, tranquil, crystalline lake, hidden away in the heart of the desert.

'Your ambitions?' he prompted.

It seemed mundane to talk about her college course after that, or the complexities of a boiler and the satisfaction of tinkering with an engine and hearing it throb into life. But that was her life, Millie thought. And she loved her life. This was Khalid's life.

'Miss Francine's been kind to you?'

'Miss Francine is the best woman in the world,' Millie exclaimed sincerely. 'More than a surrogate mother, she's been the grandmother I never knew, as well as my friend and the special person I confide in, and know I can turn to if ever there's a problem.'

'I hear she turns to you.'

'You hear a lot of things,' she remarked with amusement.

'And your ambition to be a marine engineer? You could work on my ships.'

'How many do you have?'

'Enough to keep you busy.'

Millie smiled. Khalid truly lived in another world. 'I love to see the way things work,' she admitted. 'Making them run more efficiently is my passion. A new engine is like a new friend to me. I can't rest until I know what makes them tick, and how I can help them.'

'A noble career,' he commented. 'Lucky friends, lucky engines.'

She laughed. They both laughed. He nuzzled her face in a way that felt so intimate, and then he turned Burkan and rode on.

Millie was quite open about her hopes and dreams when it came to her career, but what did she do for entertainment? he wondered, having discovered that he cared more than he should.

'I'm a bluestocking,' she said when he asked the question. 'I read, study, read some more.'

'But you must go out?'

'Are you jealous?' she asked, turning in the saddle to stare at him.

Yes, he was, he discovered. 'Would you prefer me not to be?'

'I don't think that's in your nature. You're a warrior through and through.'

She was correct. The thought of another man touching Millie roused him to a passion he wouldn't have believed.

'I love Miss Francine,' she volunteered, perhaps wanting to bring the tension level down. 'So I rarely go out during my holidays.'

'You made an exception for me?'

'Of course I did,' she said easily. 'Don't pretend you're surprised.'

'I'm not surprised. Being as devastatingly irresistible as I am—'

'You are,' she said, turning to give him a frank look. 'At least, to me.'

She was so open it twisted the knife in a heart that must turn cold towards her, to protect Millie from the reality of their respective destinies. They rode in silence for a while after that.

'During term time,' she said eventually, 'I'm far too busy studying to have time to socialise.'

He was relieved in one way, but not in another. 'You need a life, Millie.'

'I have a very good life, thank you,' she returned briskly. 'And my private life is—'

'Yours to know and mine to imagine?' he suggested in a relaxed tone.

'Exactly,' she agreed.

There was only one certainty, and that was that she was in over her head, Millie concluded. It was impossible to be this close to Khalid and not care about him, and her caring ran deep. She was falling a little more in love with him with every passing minute. It was no use pretending. She was his, and she was devoted to him. Maybe she couldn't have him long-term, but her heart didn't care about that.

'Look,' he said, distracting her.

She turned her head quickly, maybe too quickly as

she followed his pointing finger, and just for a moment she felt dizzy and disoriented. It was a strange feeling…something she'd never felt before, but her head quickly cleared in time for her to agree with him that no photographic images could ever have prepared her for the reality of an oasis. They had rounded the base of a dune, and now she could see it spread out in front of her, like a sapphire set in gold. She couldn't even see the far side, and hadn't imagined it was so big. The water was so clear she could see the dark rocks underneath. And another Bedouin tent had been erected on the sugar-sand shore. The pavilion might have come straight from her dreams with its billowing blindingly white sides set against the blue of the water and the lush of the green shrubbery.

'Swim?' Khalid suggested as Burkan began to toss his head at the scent of water. 'We all deserve it, don't you think?'

He didn't expect an answer, Millie thought as Burkan took off down the dune. She screamed, but with excitement as the big horse almost lost his footing. How they stayed on board, she had no idea. Somehow Khalid managed to control the powerful stallion as it slithered and then righted, before slithering down again, and not for one moment did she feel in any danger. Between Khalid and his big horse, which was almost like an extension of himself, she knew she was safe.

'Okay?' he asked when they finally arrived panting and snorting—she was panting, horse was snorting—on level ground.

Laughing with shock, fright, happiness and excitement, she exclaimed, 'I'm fine. That was amazing.' This adventure might be reckless, and very dangerous to her heart, but every second was blissful, and she would remember it all her life. 'I'm better than fine,' she exulted as Khalid set her safely on the ground.

'But stiff, I imagine,' he said with a keen look as she took her first staggering step.

That feeling was back, and with it an overwhelming tiredness. It had been a long ride, she reasoned. What she needed was a dip in that oasis. 'So long as I don't stay like this,' she said, laughing as she added a theatrical groan, 'I'll be okay.'

'You need that swim,' he said.

'I truly do,' she agreed as they linked fingers.

'Now, take off your clothes while I untack the horse,' he instructed, yanking her close.

'Yes, Your Majesty.' She stared up into Khalid's dark, mesmerising eyes. 'Do you have any more instructions for me?'

'I will have. You can depend on it.'

She had no doubt.

When she joined him and he gazed down at Millie's naked perfection, he thought himself the luckiest man on earth. Showing no fear of Burkan, she scratched the stallion beneath his chin, while the one-man horse, fierce and unsociable, nickered with approval.

'You've won him over,' he said. 'I'll make a Bedouin of you yet.'

'Burkan won *me* over,' Millie argued, with an approving look at his horse. 'Maybe I'll make an engineer out of you,' she added with a sideways look.

'I mine sapphires,' he reminded her, 'and so I always have need of top-notch engineers.'

'So I can tinker with your boats *and* with your engines in the mine.'

'Why not?' They both knew this was a game, and would never happen, but why not play it out? 'You can tinker with anything you want to,' he said as he brought his robe over his head and tossed it aside. Taking hold of her hand, he drew her close as he led her towards the water.

'Is this a dream?' Millie asked him of the oasis. She dipped her toes as he sprang onto Burkan's back. Swinging Millie into his arms, he rode full tilt into the chill of deep water. Millie shrieked with the shock of it, and he laughed and held her close as Burkan lunged forward and began to swim. Steering the big horse towards the shade of the overhanging palm fronds, he urged him up the bank and dismounted. Lifting Millie down, he left the stallion to crop grass and rest.

'This is heaven,' Millie exclaimed softly as she rested briefly against Burkan's side to stroke him appreciatively. 'And if it is a dream, I never want it to end.'

And neither did he, but it must, he thought.

How could she not respond to a man as brutally masculine as Khalid? And so gloriously naked. Primal instinct would always triumph over common sense, Millie concluded as Khalid looped his powerful arms around her waist. He was holding her in a tantalisingly loose grip that she could have walked away from at any time, but he knew she had no intention of going anywhere. His seduction techniques were many and various, as she had learned, and she hadn't encountered one yet that wasn't fiendishly effective.

They stood in silence for a while, but that silence was so deep and intense, she could hear both their hearts beating as one.

'I want to make love to you,' he said at last. 'I mean, really make love to you.'

'What are you saying, Khalid?' Hope filled her.

'Don't you know?'

'Not unless you say it.'

'I love being with you, Millie Dillinger,' he murmured as he nuzzled her cheek and neck.

That wasn't what she'd hoped to hear. *Get over it.* Get real, as her friends at the laundry would say. Urgent pulses of sweet pleasure were teasing her body beyond endurance. Why did she have to think further than that? Of course he wanted to make love—have sex—it was all just terminology; a choice of words. She did too. Their bodies were tuned to each other's needs, and the urge to mate wouldn't leave them alone, until they were sated.

And that dose of reality helped her emotions how?

'I want you,' she whispered as Khalid backed her towards the shade. 'So much,' she added truthfully, feeling tears sting her eyes as he lowered her to the ground.

The grass was firm and warm beneath her back after the chill of the water. Their faces were close, so close their lips were almost touching. Her mouth was kiss-bruised and tingling as her arousal grew. Knowing this, he smiled and kissed her. She was his to do with as he wished.

Lowering himself carefully, he brushed his body against hers. Anticipating his weight, his heat, his strength, was almost the best part.

'No,' he warned as she positioned herself for pleasure. 'I must protect you first—'

'I can't wait!' she protested.

'You must—'

'No!' It wouldn't be the first time with Khalid that she'd pushed the boundaries. Passion as fierce as theirs could accept no boundaries or restrictions. Drawing up her legs, she arced her hips and drew him deep. Holding him secure with her inner muscles, she worked him mercilessly. Digging her fingers into his arms, she bit his neck and shoulder, growling to express all the frustration inside her. The end came quickly in a cataclysmic release. Khalid swore viciously as he fell back on the grass, but when she turned to look at him, he was smiling.

'Animal,' he said, making it sound like the greatest compliment possible. 'What are you? A sorceress? A siren? A witch?'

'A laundress,' she said.

He laughed as he pulled her across to lie on top of him. 'A very special, and very dangerous laundress,' he observed, 'and one whose talents must never be allowed to go to waste.'

'What do you mean?'

'We need teachers in Khalifa, experts in their field who can inspire our young people. I can think of no one better than you to fill that role.'

'I'm not an expert yet,' Millie pointed out.

'But you will be,' he enthused, 'and we need you in Khalifa. We have an excellent engineering college—'

'What are you saying, Khalid?' she interrupted sharply. Couldn't he see the truth? Her future didn't lie in Khalifa. 'I have a course to finish in the UK.'

'And when you have finished, come and work for me.' The fire of desire and bold intention blazed fiercely in his eyes. Khalid was used to conquering problems, and couldn't envisage a situation that wouldn't bend to his will, Millie thought. 'We're always looking for new ideas, and ambassadors to spread the word.'

'No,' she said quietly. How could she be close to him and not part of his life? 'But thanks for the offer. I really appreciate it.' She tried her best to sound sincere, and untouched emotionally by Khalid's suggestion that she could live in his beautiful country, perhaps within a stone's throw of the palace, and not have her heart break in pieces. She didn't want to hurt him, or seem ungrateful, but neither could she face the heartache that would bring.

'My loss,' he said thoughtfully.

And mine, Millie mused.

Khalid's stroking touch was more gentle than usual as he brought her to rest on his chest, as if his thoughts were plaguing him, and he was still on the hunt for a solution. She couldn't bear it, and had to tell herself not to cry. You can't have everything you want, and nor can he, she told herself firmly. *But she only wanted this*, and it seemed so unfair that she couldn't have it, Millie thought as Khalid stroked her hair, reassuring her, as if he sensed her distress.

It was as if they were already saying goodbye, she realised. A great surge of distress accompanied this thought, and threatened to overwhelm her. She had to be strong. She would be.

They swam again, and it was lovely and cleansing, and the tiredness she'd experienced after the long ride had fallen away. But there was sadness too. After a lifetime of carefully guarding her emotions, she was finding it harder and harder to hide them, and this was beginning to feel like the final act in a play. Being alone in the desert with Khalid had undoubtedly strengthened the bond between them. Whether that was good or bad remained to be seen. Feeling like this after making love was wonderful—so why was she crying again? Millie wondered as she floated on her back in the cooling water, gazing at the sky. She had to pull herself together and fast. She'd always known they would have to go their separate ways to live their very different lives. And she would always feel different, as if part of Khalid would never leave her. A sense of rightness and completeness filled her, taking over from the tears. It was a feeling she would have to try and remember for always and ever, she accepted as she tried her best not to think about returning home.

'Come on,' Khalid prompted when she shivered involuntarily. 'You've had enough swimming for today. You must eat something now.'

'To keep up my strength?' she teased, wondering why just the mention of food should make her stomach churn.

Khalid soon made her forget. Drawing her into his arms where she felt safe, he made sure that the only hunger she felt was for him.

Don't play with fire.

Why not? Brushing away the shadows that briefly darkened her elation, she put on the fresh robe that, miraculously, or so it seemed to Millie, had been laid out on the bank for her, together with a robe for Khalid, as well as towels for both of them, and simple sandals to slip on. Millie's robe was so pretty. Diaphanous rose-coloured silk, it was a perfect foil for Khalid's stark black. What else would a hawk of the desert wear? she thought as he turned to look at her. Then it occurred to her that there must be invisible helpers, and she glanced around red-faced with embarrassment at the thought that they might have been watched. 'I thought we were alone,' she exclaimed.

'We are.' Khalid shrugged, unconcerned.

'And the gold table covered in a crisp white linen cloth?' She'd just noticed it now. 'Did Burkan set the table for us?'

'He's a horse of many talents,' Khalid told her straight-faced.

And the line of tents and portable buildings that had been erected in the shade behind the dune? How had she missed those? She'd been too preoccupied with Khalid, Millie realised. Of course the ruling sheikh of Khalifa would have staff and security wherever he went, and she was naïve for not knowing this from the start. A little more discretion would be required in future, not to mention muffling her screams of pleasure, she thought as Khalid took her by the hand.

'No one will disturb us,' he promised with a long stare into her eyes. He confirmed this with a lingering kiss, but the shadows were back. What was the point of trying to pretend they were lovers on the bank of an oasis, with nothing to stand between them and their passion, when there was an entire tented city at Khalid's beck and call, just a few yards away?

Duty first, duty always, Millie thought as he excused himself to check with his people if there were any outstanding issues to be dealt with in Khalifa before they settled down to eat.

I love you, she thought as he strode away.

Turning, she entered the royal pavilion on her own. She'd better get used to that feeling of being alone. She loved him madly, deeply, passionately, but must keep that to herself. Khalid had always made it clear where his duty lay, and, wonderful though this trip to the desert had been, their time together was almost over.

CHAPTER ELEVEN

DETERMINED TO MAKE the most of whatever time was left, Millie kept a lookout for Khalid's return. She blenched to see him arriving with a group of grandly dressed men. Quickly retreating into the private section in the depths of the pavilion, she remained by the dividing curtain to listen. It could only be a deputation from his court. Khalid brought them inside, and she could tell by the tone of his voice that he was furious.

'I gave clear instructions that I was not to be disturbed while I was in the desert. Speak in English,' he rapped when the leader of the men, with an obsequious bow, began to say something. Khalid knew she was here, and he wanted her to hear everything. It filled her with warmth and confidence to know he was protecting her even now. Though the sense that they would be parting soon hadn't left her, and her heart was aching with real physical pain.

'Forgive me, Your Majesty,' the same man said. 'Urgent news from the capital.'

'Which is?' Khalid demanded, looking every inch

the hawk of the desert as he spoke, Millie saw as she stood in the shadows.

'Another bridal party has arrived, this time from a Mediterranean kingdom—'

She heard Khalid's sound of disgust. 'Have these people no manners? Are they so desperate to offload their daughter? That's enough. They have been told not to come, and nothing has changed.'

'We know you had forbidden this, but the Mediterranean royal family decided to bring the Princess, anyway.'

'In direct contravention of my wishes.'

'Yes, Your Majesty.'

A Mediterranean princess, Millie thought. She could imagine someone beautiful, who had been groomed to rule at Khalid's side—not a tomboy with oil on her overalls. She had always known this would happen. There was no point in getting upset about it. She shouldn't feel so brutally let down. Khalid had done everything he could to protect her, and she had always known what she was getting herself into. He had never misled her for a moment. Her broken heart was all her own doing.

He was still talking, but in a muted tone, and in his own language. To her ears, he seemed calmer, happier. Perhaps the Princess was very beautiful and he'd relented. Digging her fingers into her palms until her nails cut the skin, she was glad he was talking in Khalifan. She couldn't bear to hear the truth as written by her imagination.

'Take refreshments before you go,' she heard Khalid say in English. 'I will follow you back to the palace in due course.'

She clung to the tent pole, feeling dizzy as she waited for the men to leave. Being hidden in the pavilion should have been wake-up call enough. She could only ever be hidden away. She could choose to be his mistress, even now. The offer had never been rescinded. Think of the engines she could work on, while she waited for him to find time for her.

Even humour couldn't help her now, Millie concluded; she was long past laughing at this situation. And she couldn't fudge how she felt when he came to find her.

'Millie?'

Her head was swimming. For the first time in her life, she didn't feel strong, or capable, she felt faint, physically, mentally, and it must have shown. As if alarmed by her pallor, Khalid took hold of her arm and drew her to him. The pretence was over. A prospective bride with ironclad credentials was waiting at the palace in his capital city. There was no place for Millie in Khalid's life going forward. 'I've always known this had to end,' she said, smiling as she tried to make it easy for him. 'I just didn't think it would happen so soon. But,' she added in a fiercely upbeat tone, 'better now, and quickly, than death by a thousand cuts.'

'What on earth are you talking about?' he demanded. 'Didn't you hear me send them away? This is not the end, unless you want it to be the end. We can have as long as you want.'

As his mistress, she thought. A muscle flicking in his jaw betrayed his tension as he waited for her answer.

'You've spent too long away,' she said, 'and the country is missing you. It's time for us both to go home.'

He held her at arm's length so he could stare into her face. 'I don't regret a moment of this.'

That sounded like a death knell.

Dreams, she mused as she stared into Khalid's harsh, warrior face. They all had to end somewhere, and she would never hurt him by prolonging this. How could she hurt the man she loved?

'Nothing has changed,' he insisted. 'Those men answer to me.'

'But I don't,' she said.

There was a silence, as if he needed to come to terms with the fact that she wasn't a princess to be paraded in front of him for his approval, but Millie, the laundress, soon to be engineer, who made her own decisions.

Millie could deliver a rebuke with her silent defiance more effectively than with a million words. His men would go back to the palace, and send the Princess and her family away, but the damage was done. The expression in Millie's eyes said this idyll was over, and it wasn't up to him to change the rules. He would try to persuade her she was wrong, but Millie was her own woman, and would plough her own furrow. Wealth and status meant nothing to her. She looked for more meaning that that.

'The Princess is one of many my royal council has asked me to consider. Our constitution allows the royal council to choose a bride for me—'

'What?' Millie exclaimed.

'The law didn't trouble Saif. He would have his women and his bride—'

'And you're different?' she said, feeling faint, feeling unlike herself, feeling furious.

'I will change the law,' he said.

'In time?' And when he didn't answer, she added, 'I've no intention of waiting in line to learn if you're engaged or married. I have a life too, and I need to be getting on with it. I can't postpone everything each time you decide to go back to Khalifa to trial a prospective wife.'

'I have no intention of trialling anyone—'

'Then?' she interrupted, tight-lipped.

She brought him up short, staring at him with such trust, when he knew he could offer her nothing. There would be an engagement. His country expected him to make an advantageous marriage, and he couldn't put it off for ever.

'So, it's definite, then?' she said.

He couldn't lie to her and only briskly nodded his head.

'Why prolong the agony?' she demanded, lifting her chin, strong for both of them now. 'I should go, and so should you. This is over.'

Something tore in his heart as she said the words

that needed to be spoken. 'I had planned to show you the desert.'

'As I had planned to learn more about Khalifa,' she agreed, 'but that will never happen now. I think we both have to be realistic.'

She'd come through so much. Why must he be the one to hurt her like this?

'Can you call for the helicopter, please?' she asked briskly. 'I'd like to leave now, or as soon as possible.'

He admired her so much. Nothing knocked Millie down, or, if it did, she soon bounced back again. 'I'll drop you at the airport when I leave,' he agreed stiffly, knowing she was giving them both an easy way out. But she flinched, and he supposed he must have sounded clinical. After the wild passion they'd shared the contrast to this was just too stark. But he couldn't hurt her, and the surest way of doing that was to keep her close.

'One more night,' he insisted, catching her close. 'I'm not asking your permission,' he added. 'This is a direct order. We have one more night in each other's arms.'

'No. I can't,' she said, shaking her head.

'Or, you won't?' he asked softly.

'Khalid, please, don't you think this is hard enough without spinning out the agony?'

He now proved how ruthless he could be, and seduced her.

'You don't play fair,' she complained in a shaking sigh.

'That's right, I don't,' he agreed.

* * *

The bed Khalid was backing her towards was composed entirely of down-filled pillows, covered in the softest, finest silk. In this fragrant shaded cool, he laid her down and then joined her as he continued to soothe and arouse. She knew it was wrong, but who could resist him when he lifted her and rested her buttocks on the cushions, and spread her legs wide?

'No, we mustn't,' she said, thrashing her head.

'I'd say, we must,' he argued.

'It will only make things worse,' she said as she wavered between reason and need.

'For you or for me?' he asked as he paused to protect her.

'For both of us,' she gasped against his chest as he moved over her.

It was always a shock when Khalid took her, he was so big, but he was also careful, knowing that his size was a consideration, before it became a pleasure. He'd always taken care of her, she acknowledged as he sank deep. Relaxing, she tightened her inner muscles around him to hold him firmly in place, but he had an answer for that too. Rotating his hips, he buffeted the tiny area that always needed him. 'Now,' she begged. 'Don't wait. I need this.'

Pulling back, he stared down. 'Are you ready?'

'Find out?' she said.

Bracing himself on his forearms so his weight didn't crush her, Khalid thrust his hips forward and took her in one, deep plunge to the hilt.

'Faster! Harder!' she cried to encourage him, and he

rewarded her by doing just that. Maintaining a steady rhythm, he made sure that she extracted every single pleasure pulse, before launching her into an atomic release. Even before she'd quietened, he'd turned her on her stomach. She lifted her buttocks to encourage him. Nudging her legs wider, he pressed his hand into the small of her back to raise them even more. Taking a cheek in each hand, he controlled her steady movements back and forth.

They made love through the night as if each second must be savoured, because very soon it would be their last.

'Wake up. It's time to leave.'

Millie blinked groggily as she slowly came to. At first, it seemed she didn't know where she was, only that Khalid was beside her. Groaning with contentment as the new day began, she reached for him.

'Not now,' he said, starting to get out of bed.

'Yes, now,' she argued. He'd made her insatiable. Something had changed in her body that made her need him more than ever.

'We have to leave soon,' he explained, but as their eyes met and she smiled into his, he relented. Drawing her into his arms, he kissed her with the utmost tenderness, and when he took her this time he was equally thorough and caring. 'I'm going to find it hard to be parted from you,' he admitted when they finally rested back with a contented sigh.

'But part we must,' she said, forcing brightness into her tone.

Was she laughing through her tears, or did she not care that much? This was a unique situation for him. He was always so sure of everything, but Millie was an enigma it would take a lifetime he couldn't give her to unravel.

Dropping a kiss on Khalid's shoulder, she tried to show that she could handle this. 'Shall we have one last swim?' she asked. She shrugged. 'We need to shower, so…?'

'There's no need to leave the tent,' Khalid explained. 'There's a bathing platform behind that curtain.'

'All mod cons,' she said lightly, turning to look to hide her tears. 'You've thought of everything,' she confirmed, turning back to face him as soon as she'd got her emotions under control.

'I try to,' he said, making things worse by dragging her close for a fierce, and maybe final kiss.

They linked fingers to walk the short distance across the rugs to the decorative cover he had indicated. Drawing it back revealed the shining lake of water.

'Wow,' Millie breathed. 'I'm never going to get used to this, and I'm going to miss it so much.' How much he'd never know.

'You can swim in the shallows without anyone seeing you,' Khalid said as he led her forward. 'I hope your private bathing area meets with your approval, Ms Dillinger?'

He swept her a mock bow and now those tears were threatening again. But no way was she going to weaken. They should part as friends, not discontented lovers.

All well and good, she thought as they stood in the pearly light of dawn, staring out over the most incredible panorama of waking desert and limpid oasis. If this was the last time they swam together, she was going to make the most of it and the future would have to wait.

Khalid's outstretched hand invited her to join him. They linked fingers again and walked to the water's edge. One last time, she thought as they waded in together. The water was like a warm bath, but they were silent as they swam, as if both of them knew that the time for games and laughter was done. They returned to the tent to be greeted by the delicious scent of cooked food and good coffee. A stack of clean towels and fresh robes were waiting for them. Khalid's people were discreet, and intuitive too, she thought.

'The best staff in the world,' he confirmed when she expressed her gratitude.

Removing the beautiful robe, she hung it up with care, regretting the fact, for the first time in her life, that it was back to oil-smeared overalls, and she would never wear a beautiful Khalifan robe again. She dressed quickly in travel clothes, just jeans and a top, and a sweater because it would be cold when she arrived in England. She took one last look around at the beautiful tent filled with exquisite artefacts. Even the sapphires in the gold bowls didn't trouble her now. The past was the past, and it was time to face the future.

'Do you mind if I take a picture?' she asked.

'Why?' Khalid said, frowning.

'To remember all this,' she explained.

'Will you forget so easily?'

There was hurt in his eyes. Goodness knew what he could see in hers. 'No,' she said. 'I won't forget. But when I'm an old lady, it will be nice to reminisce.'

'To remind yourself that this actually happened?'

They stared at each other, both wanting to say more, but the sound of rotor blades intruded. Perhaps as well, Millie thought. 'Is that our lift?' she said, trying to sound casual.

'Yes,' Khalid confirmed.

That single word, and the way he said it, ripped the heart from her chest and made her wonder how much more she could take without breaking down. Everything, Millie thought. She'd take everything. She was strong and would remain so. It was the only way to be.

'Are you tired of my company?' Khalid teased.

Never. She would never tire of him, never forget him, never fall out of love with him, she thought as his hawk-like stare burned steadily into hers. But she was aching with tension and needed to leave. Why prolong the agony for either of them? Khalid was as tense as she was. She had never seen him so tightly wound.

'This is torture,' she admitted.

There was a moment when they stared at each other, and the next moment she was in his arms. 'I'm not ready to part with you!' he ground out in a voice hoarse with passion.

'Then, you're not being fair,' she said. Removing herself from his arms, she stared up. 'You can't al-

ways have what you want, Your Majesty. A country
depends on you.'

Khalid had to be strong for everyone, she thought as
his hawk-like stare stabbed into hers. 'I don't want to
hurt you, Millie. You've had too much trouble in your
life, and I hold myself responsible for much of that.'

'Then, don't,' she said. 'I'm responsible for my actions. I chose to be here. I chose to listen to what you
had to tell me about my mother, and it was my decision to stay. But I've always known we can't have a
life together. Don't worry,' she added brightly, dredging up resolve from the depth of her soul. 'I won't let
history hold me back, or you, for that matter. What
we had was good, but it's done now. You have to let
me go. I mean it, Khalid,' she said when he looked
shocked. 'Let me go.'

'Are you serious? That's it? Done? Just like that?'

'I am.' She guessed he'd never been on the receiving
end of a refusal before. She continued quickly before
her heart overruled her head. 'Did you think I wouldn't
be able to live without you? I won't become your mistress. I have a good life back in England, and people
who love me. I'm working towards a job I enjoy—'

'So you don't need me,' he supplied.

'Exactly,' she confirmed with a thin smile.

'Good,' he said tonelessly. 'I could ask for nothing
more for you.'

Parting from him was the hardest thing she'd ever
had to do. Killing off all hope of a future, or recon-
ciliation was worse.

'If that's what you really want,' he said.

He had to be sure, she thought. There could be no going back now. Her next words would end this. 'It is what I want,' she said. 'We both know it's the only way forward, and best for both of us.'

That might be right, but no one could steal her memories away. They would stay with her for ever.

CHAPTER TWELVE

IT WAS BACK to earth with a bump when Millie walked into Miss Francine's laundry. She'd gone straight back to college from Khalifa, needing time alone to get her head straight, and had bunked in with a new student who asked no questions, not even when Millie had carelessly left packaging from several pregnancy tests in the bin. Bloating, feeling sick in the morning, suffering from a severe dose of emotional incontinence, as well as sore breasts, could not be ignored for ever and she'd taken her first test the week she got back. And the result was positive. All five had been positive.

Having scoured the news each day, she'd found no announcement of an engagement in Khalifa. But that meant nothing, Millie thought, as Lucy's head shot up with surprise as she walked in. Everyone was staring at her, and trying not to. They must be wondering how she felt about her time in the desert with the ruler of Khalifa. Nothing travelled faster than bad news, but confirmation of her pregnancy was the very best of news, so no one at the laundry knew about that yet, not even Miss Francine. Millie couldn't wait to tell the elderly woman who'd done so much for her that Miss Francine was about to become a grandmother. Now it was just a case of finding the right moment to inform the mighty ruler of Khalifa that he was about to become a father.

Millie and Lucy hugged warmly, and then Millie asked about Miss Francine.

'In her office,' Lucy said, adding worriedly, 'with her lawyers.'

'Lawyers?' Millie echoed with concern.

'Go and join them, and then you can tell me what's happening,' Lucy whispered so their colleagues couldn't hear. 'You're like a daughter and she's missed you. Here, let me take your things. It doesn't look good,' Lucy added with a glance at the firmly closed door to Miss Francine's office.

'Millie!'

Lucy was right. Miss Francine couldn't have been more relieved, or happier to see her, but Millie was disturbed to see how frail she looked. She could feel her ribs through the thin cardigan and blouse as they embraced. When they parted, Miss Francine introduced Millie to the two lawyers sitting in front of the desk. 'Mr Frostwick's firm has worked in my best interest for years,' she explained to Millie, 'but I've given him a real problem this time.'

'Can you tell me about it?' Millie asked her old friend gently, with an enquiring look at the two men. What could have gone so badly wrong while she was away?

Miss Francine lost no time explaining. 'I've been

advised by my doctors to retire from the business with immediate effect. And with no one to take over from me...' She spread her arms wide. 'Millie is studying to be a marine engineer, you know,' she told the Frostwick team with all the warmth of a proud mother.

'I'm on holiday from college, so I can stay and help out,' Millie offered.

'It might not be enough,' the older of the two lawyers commented gruffly.

'And I won't hear of it,' Miss Francine said, closing that avenue down. 'You've worked too hard to give up now.'

'I'm not talking about giving up, just taking a longer break,' Millie soothed.

'The business will have to be sold,' the lawyer cut in. 'There's no money to save it,' he added bluntly, 'unless you have a suggestion,' he said as he stared at Millie.

If the business was sold, Miss Francine's name would be lost, Millie thought, and a lifetime's work would count for nothing. 'Could the name be retained, perhaps?'

The flash of hope in her old friend's eyes stabbed Millie in the heart. She could come up with as many suggestions as she liked, but if only money would save the laundry—

'I'm afraid the name can't be kept if an offer is accepted from one of the big chains,' the lawyer was saying, crashing into her thoughts, 'and the creditors will insist on a sale. There's been a lot of interest,' he continued on a brighter note. 'Miss Francine's reputation is second to none—'

'Of course it is,' Millie interrupted, seeing how distressed her elderly friend was becoming. Millie had been too young to help her mother, but nothing would get in the way of helping Miss Francine. 'I'll sort it out,' she said in a tone that brooked no argument. 'And now I think Miss Francine needs to rest.'

'Of course,' the lawyers agreed, standing up. 'We'll be in touch.'

'Don't worry,' she told Miss Francine as soon as the door had closed behind the visitors. 'I meant what I said.'

Miss Francine gave a grateful smile, which at the same time seemed to accept there was nothing *to* be done. Millie had other ideas. There was one person with enough money to put this right, and, after everything Miss Francine had done for Millie, she was going to enlist his help.

Ask Khalid for money when she'd broken off with him? See him again? Speak to him? He wouldn't even take her calls. He'd wanted a clean break too.

She wouldn't let Miss Francine down. Her elderly friend deserved a far better end to her working life than this. She didn't waste any time placing the call to Khalid. The sooner she got it over with, the sooner she could…well, if not exactly relax, at least satisfy herself that she'd tried every avenue.

Khalid answered on the second ring. She might have thought he'd been waiting for her call, if his comment hadn't been quite so crisp and short. 'I'll send transport for you,' he said.

'That's not what I want,' Millie said tensely. 'I'm

not coming back to Khalifa.' She drew a deep, steadying breath. 'I'm asking for your help.'

'Money?' he said flatly.

'But not for me,' Millie said quickly, going on to explain the situation.

'Is money all you want?'

'Should there be anything more?' Of course there should! She had to tell him about the baby— Over the phone? No. She couldn't do that to him.

'Anything more?' he queried. In the pause that followed, she could picture him frowning.

'No. There's nothing more,' she confirmed, knowing she could never agree to his terms. Becoming Khalid's mistress while he lived with an arranged bride would break her, and that was even supposing he hoped for something more.

Millie's heart was in pieces to hear Khalid sounding so unemotional. It was as if he hadn't missed her at all—and why should he? They were still worlds apart, Millie concluded sadly, not only in the physical sense, separated by thousands of miles, but by a yawning gulf in their destiny. But she couldn't allow any of that to matter now. She had to try and do a deal with him, to save Miss Francine's laundry. Taking a deep, steadying breath, she hit him with her first idea.

'Would you have any objection to my putting Miss Francine's lawyer in touch with your Development Grant department? I thought that perhaps they could look at the possibility of franchising the business,' she went on. 'It would mean everything to Miss Francine to keep the name.'

'And she could be a figurehead?' the deep, husky voice at the other end of the line said thoughtfully.

'Exactly,' Millie agreed, relieved that he'd caught on so fast. She smiled to herself, thinking, when did the hawk of the desert ever have any difficulty in making a decision?

'I'll think about it, and let you know,' he said.

The line cut abruptly. She stared at the receiver in her hand, and only then realised that tears were streaming down her face.

Millie, Millie, Millie. Just the sound of her voice was enough for him to start cancelling appointments. Since the moment they'd parted, he'd realised that there was only one woman he could ever care for. To be a better man than his brother meant leading by example. It took time to effect change in an ancient constitution like that of Khalifa, but alterations would be made. On that he was determined.

He had omitted to mention to Millie the fact that he was in England. An invitation to dine with royalty in London at the palace tomorrow night to discuss various matters had prompted this visit. After talks and a dinner, a ball was to be held in his honour. Anticipating hopeful parents with a daughter to offload, he had planned to make his excuses and leave the palace before the ball. Hearing Millie's voice again had changed that decision.

Impatiently knuckling away tears, Millie replaced the receiver in its nest. There was no point cradling it, as if that could keep Khalid close. She had to be patient and wait to see if he would be as good as his word. She believed franchising Miss Francine's laundry would be a good investment, and could only hope that he agreed. But now she had work to do. Sprucing up the laundry to entice any investor was essential. She owed it to Miss Francine to make sure the business looked its best.

Everyone at the laundry was only too eager to repay Miss Francine's kindness by pitching in to touch up paintwork in rooms that hadn't been decorated for years. Millie's job was to check the machinery was working smoothly, and when they finished Miss Francine had promised a special supper to celebrate what she was already calling 'a new era' in the laundry's history, as if the deal to save it were already done.

Much to Millie's relief, her elderly friend seemed to have regained her former vigour, and brightened even more when Millie mentioned another idea she'd come up with, which was for Miss Francine to invite some of the workers to move into her spare bedrooms, much as Millie herself had done after her mother's death. Miss Francine was known for her soft heart, and many of the girls had experienced unpleasantness in their past like Millie. This would not only provide those who needed it with stability, but would give Miss Francine company and a little extra cash.

When their long day had finally ended, Miss Francine hurried out of the office with a printout in her hand. 'This has just arrived from the Sheikh's office,' she explained in a voice trembling with hope. 'His business development team is coming here to look us over!'

'That's wonderful,' Millie exclaimed as excitement rose around her.

Khalid hadn't let her down.

Maybe jobs would be saved, and the name of the laundry kept intact. The expression in Miss Francine's eyes was so full of happiness that it took hold of Millie's heart and twisted it hard.

'Do you really think we'll be okay?' she asked Millie.

'I know we will,' Millie said confidently as she plucked the pencil out of her up-do to tick another job off her list.

Everyone was laughing at each other's paint-streaked faces, especially at Millie's face, as she had added a good dose of black, greasy oil, and not just to her face, but all over the dungarees she'd been wearing to work on the boiler.

'I need to check one more thing,' Millie said as she climbed back into the tiny, spider-infested cubbyhole where the ancient boiler was housed. She would clean it out, once she had a minute—if that ever happened, Millie thought, grimacing as she stared around in the gloom. Brushing a web out of her hair, she checked the valve she'd replaced was working smoothly, and then carefully backed out of the confined space on all fours.

'Phew, it's hot in there,' she exclaimed as she emerged into the light. 'I'll have to set up a fan or something before the Sheikh's team arrives—'

It was the silence that alerted her to something out of the ordinary. Standing, she turned around. *'Khalid?'*

Millie's stomach clenched alarmingly and, turning away, she was forced to put her hand over her mouth.

One. Two. Three. Time up! Turn around.

'We were only speaking on the phone an hour or so ago,' she exclaimed heatedly, as if he were in the wrong. 'How on earth did you get here so quickly?'

'I'm overwhelmed by my welcome,' he said dryly.

His smoky, mocking tone, and those eyes…those all-seeing, darkly amused eyes, made her heart beat off the scale.

Was he really here? Their baby! How would he take it? I love you—so, so much. Oh, good grief, what do I look like with webs in my hair and oil on my face? I never thought to see you again, and now you're here—

And breathe.

'No! Don't touch me!' she yelped, backing away as Khalid, looking like the master of the sexual universe in a rugged jacket and jeans, advanced. 'I'm covered in oil and spiders' webs.'

As she spoke the room cleared as Miss Francine quickly ushered everyone out.

There was no stopping Khalid now. Closing the distance between them in a single step, he took hold of her arms in a non-negotiable grip, and, blazing a fierce look into her eyes, he demanded, 'Do you really think I care about a few spiders' webs?'

'You should—I mean, your expensive jacket—'

He snarled something in Khalifan that needed no translation, and dipped his head; he savaged her mouth with a kiss so deep, so firm and passionate, she almost swooned in his arms. When he let her go there was a moment she would never forget, when they stared at each other. So many frustrated hopes and dreams must be reflected in her eyes, while his were stonily determined. 'I can't do this again,' she whispered.

'Yes, you can,' he said. 'And you will.'

He was to marry some suitable princess. Why pretend? Millie's heart had already been dashed to pieces on the harsh rock of reality. But that didn't stop her heart aching with love, even as the more sensible part of her wished they could have remained continents apart, so she would never have to go through the grief of losing him again.

'You're coming with me,' he rapped.

'No, I'm not,' she argued, incredulity ringing in her voice.

'That wasn't a suggestion,' Khalid assured her. 'We've wasted enough time. Do you want my help or not?'

'At the laundry?' she said in confusion. 'Of course, I want your help. But not if you're blackmailing me— I'll find some other way.' She stared at him tensely. They had to get this straight.

Neither was prepared to back down, or give in. They were perfectly matched, she thought a little wistfully.

'You have a decision to make,' Khalid told her.

Think—think straight—make the right call.

She only had one shot at this. A lifetime of work had gone into the laundry, as well as all the precious lives Miss Francine strived so hard to put back on track. It wasn't just jobs at stake here, but people's futures and their happiness, and maybe even survival for some of her friends. She had to get this right. It wasn't about her feelings for Khalid, or even for her own self-respect; it was a bigger decision than all of that.

'Where are you going from here?' she asked tensely.

'To my London home,' Khalid told her succinctly, his eyes stern, his mouth firm.

Well, that wasn't too bad. It wasn't as far away as Khalifa. 'Can't we talk here?'

With a sound of impatience, *Sheikh* Khalid—for she could think of him as nothing else now, and in this setting—raked his hair. 'I can't just book into the local motel.'

He had a point.

'You wanted to discuss Miss Francine's case,' he reminded her. 'And *you* convinced me this meeting can't wait. *I* can't wait,' he added in a clipped tone. 'I have a country to run, and business at the palace in London. Either you come with me now, or I return to the capital without you, in which case you can go through the usual channels to apply for the grant.'

Millie's jaw dropped. 'You *are* blackmailing me.'

'I'm telling you how it is,' Khalid stated without emotion, though there was fire burning behind his eyes.

So much for romantic reunions, Millie thought, feeling her spirits dip even as her determination to do something right strengthened. 'I'll have to change my clothes—'

'No time,' he rapped. 'Everything will be waiting

for you when we arrive. Go and say goodbye to your friends.'

Millie's mind was in turmoil. This was crazy. She was still getting over the shock of seeing him. And coming to terms with how much she'd missed him, she silently admitted. Khalid's stern expression held nothing but impatience, though his kiss had suggested he was pleased to see her, she accepted wryly. If she had a chance of saving Miss Francine's business, she didn't have a choice, and better she told him about the baby when they had some prospect of privacy in his London home. 'Ten minutes,' she said.

'Five,' he countered.

She fired a look into Khalid's fierce dark eyes, to let him know she'd do this, but was no pushover. He held her stare locked in his, and in that split second she knew there would be trouble ahead. Putting down her tool bag, she headed into the next room to break the news that she was leaving to her employer and friends.

CHAPTER THIRTEEN

NOTHING IN KHALID'S life was slow or ordinary, Millie accepted as she ducked down beneath the rotor blades before climbing into his helicopter. Having seen her harness was correctly fixed and her headphones in place, he took the pilot's seat, and before she knew it they were soaring over London.

Green areas were at a premium in the centre of the city, but the Sheikh of Khalifa owned a very large swathe of green, with an impressive dwelling, a palace, really, set like a jewel in the middle of the most fabulous grounds. There was even a lake, she noticed, and as the aircraft swooped lower she could see the bustle of a big city beyond his perimeter walls. The haven inside those walls reminded her of an oasis in the middle of a glass and concrete city.

What else did she expect of the hawk of the desert? Millie wondered as Khalid hovered the aircraft over the helipad set in a courtyard the size of two football pitches, before landing it precisely in the centre of the cross.

His voice came through the speakers. 'The building dates from Tudor times,' he said as he closed down the engines.

At least he seemed to have relaxed. 'I'm impressed,' she said truthfully.

'Wait until you see inside,' he added as the engines fell silent.

Khalid was right about the inside of the building. It was the most spectacular interior she'd ever seen. It was a disappointment when he didn't offer her a tour, and simply handed her over to the care of a smiling housekeeper.

She had thought they'd have some time together, Millie reflected as he jogged up the stairs. When was she going to tell him about the baby? Would she have to make an appointment to see him? This entrance hall was so grand, with its vaulted ceiling and acres of marble floor, that she felt like a very tiny cog in the huge engine of his life.

But the housekeeper was friendly as she escorted Millie to her suite of rooms. To her *fabulous* suite of rooms, Millie amended, trying not to overreact at each new revelation. While meticulous attention had been paid to ancient architectural detail, every gizmo and tech advancement was available to make life easy, though, of course, discreetly hidden away, she saw as the housekeeper opened a drawer in an antique chest to show her the controls for lighting and blinds, and heating and air con.

'You should be comfortable,' the housekeeper said with monumental understatement. 'And if there's anything more you need, please don't hesitate to call on the house phone.' Which was also cunningly concealed in a drawer in the nightstand.

Old English panelling gleamed with loving care, while Millie's feet sank into soft rugs as she stared around. She had loved the rich, vibrant colours of the desert, but she loved these muted pastels just as much.

'I hope you like your accommodation,' the housekeeper said warmly as Millie stared up at the colourful frescoes and took in the intricate plasterwork, and walls covered with silk, rather than paper or paint.

'I love it,' Millie enthused. 'These are the most beautiful rooms I've ever seen.'

'There's a view to the lake,' the housekeeper revealed as she drew the floating voile drapes aside.

'This is just exquisite,' Millie breathed as she trailed her fingertips across the top of a mahogany dressing table. And a world away from what she was used to. It only made the gap between her and Khalid seem wider.

'I ordered the scents—' she'd been trailing her fingertips across, Millie realised now, drawing her hand back fast as the housekeeper mentioned them '—from our most famous store in London. I wasn't sure of your taste, so I hope you like at least one of them?'

'I like all of them, and thank you for your trouble.' As gilded cages went, this surely had to be one of the most opulent and refined, though it was hard to see this as a cage or a trap. Khalid's housekeeper couldn't have been nicer. Any guest would feel welcome here.

'Nothing is too much trouble for His Majesty's guests, Ms Dillinger.'

And this was said so warmly it wasn't easy to think Millie was just the most recent in a long line of His Majesty's female guests. 'I'm sure not,' she agreed, returning the housekeeper's smile.

The tour continued into the bathroom, and then into a fully fitted dressing room.

'I have also taken the liberty of ordering a number of gowns for you to choose from for the ball tomorrow night.'

'The ball?' Millie queried. She gazed in incredulity at the glittering collection of fabulous gowns.

'His Majesty has been invited as guest of honour to a ball at the palace tomorrow evening,' the housekeeper explained. 'He thought you might like to accompany him.'

Millie was speechless. At first, she thought, I'd be like a fish out of water. But then she remembered her friends at the laundry. They'd give their eye teeth to take a look around the palace, and she could tell them about it when she returned to King's Dock.

'I can't thank you enough for all the trouble you've gone to,' she told the housekeeper.

'Don't thank me, thank His Majesty—who sends his regrets, but he has business to attend to for the rest of the day and evening, and so he will meet you tomorrow evening at the ball.'

No chance to talk to him about the baby before then?

Arriving at the palace without an escort tomor-

row night seemed an insignificant challenge com-
pared to that.

'Would you like me to send up some food?' the
housekeeper asked as she prepared to leave.

The mere thought of food was enough to make Millie's stomach churn. 'Some water would be nice.'

'And a light meal, surely?' the kindly housekeeper
pressed.

She had to force herself to say, 'Thank you, that
would be lovely.'

'Call down on the house phone if you need anything
else. It's manned twenty-four hours a day, but there's
iced water in the fridge in your dressing room, as well
as a selection of soft drinks and snacks.'

Soft drinks and snacks? Millie's stomach turned
over. In her current condition, fatty, sweet things were
as attractive a prospect as a stomach bug at the ball, but
she thanked the housekeeper with a warm smile, and
when she'd left, walked into the bathroom to splash
her face with cold water. Staring into the mirror, she
knew she had to tell Khalid now. It couldn't wait. Not
if she wouldn't see him until the ball.

'I need to contact His Majesty,' she told the impersonal voice on the other end of the house phone.

'I will inform his PA, madam. Is there anything
else?'

'No. Thank you.'

She sat by the phone, and didn't have long to wait.
'Millie?'

'Khalid! Thank goodness.'

'Is something wrong?'

'No, but I need to talk to you, and not over the phone.'

'I thought the housekeeper would explain that I'm tied up.'

'She did, and I'm sorry to call, but—'

'Is it something urgent or can it wait?'

For nine months, Millie thought. Her blood was beginning to boil. Khalid had never had any difficulty making time for her when he'd wanted her in his bed. For the sake of the child inside her, she bit back her angry words. 'It's nothing urgent,' she confirmed.

'Then, I'll see you at the ball,' he said, sounding vaguely irritated.

'Until tomorrow night,' she agreed, directing this to an already dead line.

He had been granted the singular honour of standing next to the ruling monarch of the United Kingdom to receive the guests, but all he could think about was Millie. Their reunion had been disjointed and unsatisfactory, and now their second meeting would be carried out in front of a crowd. He hadn't realised how much he'd missed her until they were standing in front of each other and he'd stared down into that intelligent, combative, beautiful oil-stained face. He loved everything about her, even the pencil sticking out of her hair.

As good manners demanded, he returned his attention to the line of guests as they moved at a snail's pace in front of him, but his attention kept straying to the grand entrance doors to the ballroom, with impeccably dressed attendants flanking them at either side. Millie would appear at the top of that gracious sweep of marble steps.

He hoped.

Each new arrival was announced before being escorted down the stairs by their companion. Millie had no one to do that. He had hoped to return to his London home to surprise Millie and escort her to the ball, but his meetings had run over. They were too important to miss when the future of Khalifa depended on their outcome.

He turned as his aide whispered in his ear, 'Ms Dillinger has arrived, Your Majesty.'

'Excellent,' he murmured, instantly on high alert.

From that moment on it was an ordeal to greet the guests politely and give them his full attention, when all he wanted to do was hunt for Millie. How frustrating, he thought with some irony, that of all the many things available to him, the one thing he wanted most was out of reach.

Light blazing from countless chandeliers had momentarily blinded Millie. When her vision adjusted, she took in the glittering throng in the ballroom, resplendent with light and gilding, and the glittering jewels of the guests. A vaulted ceiling stretched a dizzying height above her head, and was decorated with the most exquisite colourful frescoes. An orchestra was already seated, and waiting for the instruction to play. Even with these distractions, she needed no prompting to find Khalid. Her gaze flew to him like a heat-seeking missile, and as he turned to look at her she wasn't disappointed.

But had she chosen the right dress?

Maybe not…everyone was staring at her, and a hush had fallen over the ballroom. Feeling exposed, she reviewed her choice of gown. She'd been careful not to choose anything too brightly coloured, or low-cut, or tight-fitting, and definitely not white. She didn't want Khalid getting the wrong idea. She needed his help at the laundry, and had to focus on that. She had to tell him about their child, and still dreamed that when she did he would be as excited as she was at the prospect of creating a new life.

The dress, Millie reminded herself as her name was announced and she started down the stairs. *It was fine.* Careful as she was, she'd still had a wide choice of gowns, and had chosen a dream of a dress in a subtle shade of forest green, for no better reason than it reminded her of the lush banks of the oasis. Composed of floating lightweight silk chiffon, over a foundation of the same shade, it was covered in tiny crystals that shimmered beneath the light of countless chandeliers, like sunlight on the ripples of a lake. It fitted her like a glove, but as she wouldn't be able to wear a close-fitting gown for much longer she'd looked at herself in the mirror before setting out, and thought, Why not?

Millie's presence had caused an electric response in the ballroom. Everyone felt it as they stared towards the entrance where she stood. She had no need of diamond tiaras or a royal title to cause a buzz. Her warm

smile to the footman who'd shown her in said everything about Millie. She made people want to get to
know her, and for her to share some of that magic
dust. She was more than a beauty, she was a kind and
lovely woman, and even as Khalid was thinking this
an ambassador leaned across to ask him if he knew
her. He was about to answer when an upstart prince
seized his opportunity and, leaving the receiving line,
strode at speed towards Millie, no doubt intending to
escort her the rest of the way down the stairs.

She's mine!

The thought hit him like a freight train.

'Excuse me, Your Majesty… Ambassador—' A
brisk dip of his head, and he'd left the line to chase
after the Prince. Guests fell back at his approach, but
his stare remained fixed on his goal.

Millie watched as the crowd below her on the dance
floor parted like the Red Sea, first to admit the royal
Prince, and then a tall, brutally masculine man in
flowing black robes.

Khalid *and* the young man she didn't recognise
were both heading her way!

Something made the younger man turn around.
Seeing Khalid, he glanced at Millie. Quickly assess-
ing the situation, he stepped back. 'You're a lucky
man,' he said as the hawk of the desert swept past him.

Riveted by the drama, the crowd now turned to
stare at Millie. She was halfway down the stairs, and
had no alternative but to stand and watch. Or did she?
Taking one of her famous executive decisions, she continued on down the stairs.

Khalid waylaid her. 'Take care,' he instructed, 'or you might tumble in those high heels. You look fabulous, by the way.'

For an instant, it was such a thrill to see him, hear him, smell him, touch him—and he was right about the risk of her tumbling down the stairs, while she was distracted by him—she didn't say a word. But then, making another executive decision, she placed her hand on his steadying arm. Fire streaked through her. She smiled. She should have known the effect he would have on her. 'Shouldn't you be with the royal party?' she asked, struggling to maintain her dignity while her body insisted on behaving with no dignity at all.

Touching Khalid sent pulses of excitement racing through her. This was the father of her child? It hardly seemed possible. The same man who didn't know yet, Millie reminded herself. The thought was like taking an ice-bath. She would tell him as soon as she could. It was important to let him know she wanted nothing from him.

But she smiled and the ball went on. No one, not even Khalid knew the thoughts in her head tonight. Taking his cue from their arrival on the dance floor, the conductor turned to the orchestra and raised his baton.

The rest of the night passed in a series of images she would never forget. A ball at the palace was everything she had dreamed it might be and more. The food was delicious, the music was sublime, and Khalid was... too perfect, at least for her, and that made her heart ache more than ever.

Being the Sheikh of Khalifa's guest was like holding the golden ticket, Millie discovered. Everyone
greeted her with warmth, and a rustle of interest followed them around the ballroom. It was a very different world, and she appreciated the chance to be here,
but tucked away inside her enjoyment of the evening
was the niggling suspicion that people assumed she
was just another conquest of an immensely powerful man.

'You're not fooled by any of this, are you?' Khalid
remarked with his customary intuition as he escorted
her to his table.

'Can you read my thoughts?'

'Always,' he said.

Now she knew that wasn't true, and smiled, relaxing. 'I keep some thoughts hidden,' she admitted.

'And I wouldn't change you,' he said in a serious
tone as he waved the palace attendant away so he
could hold her chair himself. 'I like you just the way
you are.'

Their eyes met briefly, and Khalid's stare was so
direct, she thought this was the moment to tell him—in
a crowded ballroom, full of people who would love to
overhear what they said? It would have to wait. 'Will
you stay much longer?' she asked instead.

'I'm in your hands.'

That comment was no help at all. And then the rest
of the dinner guests joined them, and it was impossible
to get away, so she sat and talked and ate and danced,
as if everything were as it should be.

When the royal party left, it was a sign that everyone else could leave, but she had to be sure that Khalid wouldn't disappear again when they reached his London home. 'Can we talk when we get back?' she pressed as he escorted her out of the ballroom.

'Of course,' he reassured her with a slight frown. 'I hadn't forgotten you wanted to speak to me.'

Though he could have no idea about the subject of that talk, she thought as he helped her into the rear seat of the royal limousine, with its flag of Khalifa flying proudly from the roof. And a uniformed chauffeur seated only feet away from them, which made confidential conversation impossible.

'You're very quiet,' Khalid commented as they drove smoothly through the London streets. Raising the privacy panel between them and the driver, he turned to face her. 'What's wrong, Millie?'

'I'm just tired,' she said, unable to meet his eyes. Telling him such momentous news in the back of a car, however grand, didn't sit with her any better than in a crowded ballroom.

'And you look quite pale,' he observed as the street lights flickered across her face. 'But I don't buy you being tired. You were the star of the ball. Adrenalin must be pumping through your veins.'

And it was, Millie thought, but for all the wrong reasons. After the intimacies they'd shared, telling Khalid that she was pregnant should have been the easiest thing on earth, but instead it was turning out to be the hardest.

'What is this mystery?' he asked. There was a pause, and then he said, 'Are you pregnant?'

Millie gave an audible gasp. Never one to shirk the truth, she could do no more than admit, 'Yes, I am.' She could only wait for his reaction and play off that, but Khalid remained silent until they reached his London home, where he helped her out of the limousine as if he'd learned nothing unusual that night, and ushered her up the steps with his usual care.

'Ten minutes,' he said, turning to face her when his butler opened the door.

She watched him jog up the magnificent mahogany staircase. He didn't look round, and there was no offer of a steadying hand. It should have been a relief to have her wonderful news out in the open, but instead she felt more diminished than ever as she stood in the magnificent vaulted hall.

Rubbish! She was about to become a mother. And that took guts. This was no time for feeling anything other than confident about the future. Once she had reassured Khalid she wouldn't make any call on him, he was sure to see she meant it and be relieved.

A child. They were having a child. Shocked at the enormity of this turn of events, he was fiercely excited. A baby was the natural consequence of so much sex, he reflected, and however careful he'd been, there had been times…

Releasing his grip on the back of the chair, he began to pace his study. He needed time to think. Ten minutes wasn't long enough. This was as much emotion as he'd ever felt. Having grown up in a home where displays of emotion were frowned upon, his older brother, Saif, had been indulged, while Khalid, as the younger son, and by far the more spirited child, had largely been ignored, and consigned to the care of servants. By the age of seven he had learned not to yearn for the love of his parents, and had known that he would have to make his own way in the world. He'd studied hard to be the best he could be, and had gone on to serve his country in the forces, before going into business. Saif had never shown any interest in the sapphire mines, only in spending the money they produced, so it had been up to Khalid to bail out the royal treasury.

Duty remained as vital to him now as it had been then. The chance to have anything more than a formal royal life had never occurred to him, but before he could reassure Millie, he must open Pandora's box. He had no option now, but telling her everything about that night was a risk. It could destroy her; destroy all the trust she'd built and the confidence she'd gained. Withholding the truth would almost certainly drive her away from him, but he would never contemplate building a child's future on lies and evasion.

Having received the call to join Khalid in his study, she knew after he'd only been talking for a few minutes why he had wanted to keep things formal between them. 'Let me get this straight,' she said, holding up a hand to silence him. 'You've been receiving reports on me since that night?' She hated the way her voice quavered with shock.

'Every school report,' he confirmed evenly, as if

this were completely normal, 'and every course you ever took. Every friend you made—'

'How *dare* you snoop on me like that?' she demanded, incensed.

'You were made an orphan that night,' he continued, ignoring her outburst, 'and I hold myself responsible for that. I felt protective towards you from the start, and I couldn't just turn my back on you and walk away.'

'So you paid for everything throughout my entire life.' He remained silent.

'You thought it your duty,' she guessed bitterly.

'Miss Francine was more than eager to give you a home,' he argued in the same calm tone. 'She was already very fond of you, but that isn't an excuse for either of us to expect an elderly woman to bear the additional cost of housing you.'

'I never did,' Millie exploded. How dared he suggest such a thing? 'I always paid my way.'

'Yes, you did,' he agreed, 'but Miss Francine's finances were perilously balanced, and she still refused to take any money from me. The least I could do was cover your education.'

'So my scholarships—'

'You earned every one of them,' he stated firmly. 'Khalifa does not bestow grants where they are not deserved.'

'Khalifa?' One shock on top of another. 'I thought my awards came from the college. There was never any mention of Khalifa.'

'Nothing is ever done in Khalifa to garner public acclaim. Everything is low-key.'

The way he liked it, she thought, still trying to come to terms with the fact that Khalid of Khalifa had been a major player in her life since the day of her mother's tragic death.

There was a question she had to ask him. 'Was it guilt that made you do this?'

'Partly, yes,' he admitted.

'I would rather you'd told the truth to the court, than be here now.'

'I did tell the truth to the court.'

He had just left a lot out, knowing it would make the headlines and those headlines would live for ever, taunting Millie with the truth of her mother's death.

'You told your version of the truth,' she accused him.

'Doesn't everyone?' He opened his arms wide. 'The truth is always open to interpretation.'

'Not in my world,' she shot back bitterly.

'Some facts aren't helpful, Millie.'

'Like those that prove your brother guilty of murder?' she suggested with a short, humourless laugh.

'Someone else pushed your mother. I told you that it was her dealer.'

'But your brother drove my mother to the edge—he held that party—his guests mocked my mother. Whatever your lawyers said in court about my mother's fate being in her own hands—her own *shaking* hands,' she added hotly, 'surely someone could have saved her! *You* should have saved her! I should have—'

'You're torturing yourself unnecessarily,' he said as she broke off.

'Says the man who fathered my child!' she raged.

'You lied to me, Khalid. You've been lying to me since the day the *Sapphire* sailed back into King's Dock. I should have gone with my gut then, and stayed away from you.'

'Your gut told you to see me,' he argued quietly. 'And you did the right thing. You've never turned your back on a problem yet, so why start now?'

'Some things are better avoided? And you're one of them! Why couldn't you just tell me that you were going to be part of my life?'

'Would you have preferred me to feed the scandal sheets?'

'I would have preferred the truth,' she flared. 'It makes me wonder what else you're hiding,' she added with an acid glare. 'You saved your brother—'

'To prevent my country from being dragged through the mire,' he defended. 'After that was done, it was all about you.'

'And I'm expected to believe that.' Turning her back, she folded her arms, as if to contain her emotions. 'Well, now it's about me and my child,' she said, whirling around to confront him, 'which must be a considerable inconvenience for you.'

'It's nothing of the sort,' he assured her.

She threw him a sceptical look. 'I can just imagine the headlines: The Sheikh and the laundress expecting a baby, after the ruler of Khalifa returns to the UK to seduce the daughter of his brother's victim.'

'A rather long headline,' he observed, curbing his natural response. He knew it was hormones driving this rant, but that didn't make it acceptable.

'Don't make a joke of this,' she warned.

'And don't you live in the past. We have a child to consider now, and the future of that child is far more important than anything that's happened to us previously.'

Her lip trembled, and now he regretted pulling her up short. But not too much. What he had said was true.

'I'm sorry,' she said. 'I don't know why I thought I could discuss this with you calmly.'

'Because you can.'

'So long as I toe your line?'

'So long as you state your case clearly and I state mine. Now. It's been a long day for both of us. May I suggest we reconvene this meeting in the morning?' Before she could answer, he stood up and walked to the door. Opening it, he waited for her to leave. After a moment's hesitation, she did so.

'Nine o'clock tomorrow morning on the terrace for breakfast,' he said.

Lifting her chin, she walked past him without another word.

CHAPTER FOURTEEN

KHALID HAD BEEN watching over her all these years? Millie didn't know whether to be comforted or furious. Back in the beautiful suite of rooms that had been allocated to her in his London home, she was consumed by blind fury and hormones—and blind fury was definitely winning out.

She'd told him they were expecting a child, and his response had been that they'd talk about it in the morning? What was that about? This was the biggest thing that had ever happened to her: a baby, a family, a ready-made grannie in the shape of Miss Francine, and honorary aunts galore. She didn't need any more time to think about it, and she got his message loud and clear. He wasn't interested.

He thought she was overwrought? Just let him try and pay her off. Then he'd see her angry. No one was going to put a price on her baby. Wrenching her ball gown this way and that, she now discovered that the zip was out of reach. Forced to concede defeat, she realised she'd have to ask a maid to help her.

At one o' clock in the morning?

She couldn't ask anyone to get out of bed to help her undress. Glancing at the house phone—*palace* phone, Millie amended, rejigging her thoughts—she remembered the housekeeper said it was manned twenty-four hours a day. If they'd tell her where the office was, she could go there and ask whoever was on duty to give her a hand.

Lifting the receiver, she waited for the call to connect. 'Hello, I'm—'

'Millie?'

She would have known that dark, husky voice anywhere. Why was Khalid manning the phones? 'Are you monitoring my calls now?' She sounded like a shrew with a nail in its pad.

A shrew with a hawk watching her?

Everyone knew what happened when a hawk watched a shrew.

'Can't you sleep?' Khalid sounded amused.

'Can't you?' she countered.

'I happened to be passing the office, and was alerted to a call from your room. Is there something wrong?'

'Nothing you can put right,' she assured him.

She had to calm down, Millie realised as the silence stretched on. Her hormones might be racing out of control, but she was a guest here and Khalid was her host, as well as the father of her child, *and* the best hope she had to save the laundry. And she could hardly blame him for her getting stuck in her ball gown. 'It's a practical matter,' she admitted crisply.

'Like you want a cheese sandwich?' he suggested with genuine interest. 'Being pregnant these urges are natural. The kitchens are open. Just call down—or I can put you through, if you like…?'

'If you must know—' and now she felt incredibly foolish '—I can't get out of my dress.'

'I'm sure I can help with that,' he said.

Before she had chance to argue the line cut, and seconds later, or so it seemed to Millie, who was pacing up and down, there was a knock on the door, and Khalid strode in.

'Do come in,' she flared.

He laughed. Why did he have to do that? She could never resist his laugh. He'd obviously taken a shower as soon as he got back, as his hair was damp. He had changed into casual clothes, jeans and a top. That was her clue. He couldn't sleep, either.

'It didn't take you long to get here,' the shrew inside her observed. 'Were you monitoring my door, as well as the phone?'

'Turn around,' he instructed calmly.

Khalid's fingers on the back of her neck were incendiary devices to her senses, creating delicious little shocks that went streaking through her veins.

Okay, so she'd let him help her with the zip, but then he must leave.

'You're very tense tonight, Millie.'

Well, that shouldn't come as a surprise to either of them, she thought as Khalid's hands rested on her shoulders.

'You were a sensation at the ball,' he commented.

'I think the company I kept made sure of that.'

'I disagree,' Khalid argued as he pushed the dress

from her shoulders. 'You needed no help. You have your own very unique appeal.'

She stepped out of the dress, and was in his arms before she knew it. And now she was lost. One of the more enjoyable side effects of pregnancy was that it made her mad for sex.

'I can manage now, thank you,' she said primly, attempting to push him away, but her voice sounded hoarse and unconvincing. And when Khalid's arms were wrapped around her, escape was…incidental.

'I'm sure you can manage,' he agreed. 'The question is, do you want to?'

'You not going to dictate terms just because I'm pregnant,' she warned.

'And neither will you,' he assured her in a soft seductive whisper, with his mouth so close to the back of her neck she could feel his warm breath on her skin.

'What are you saying?' she demanded, reclaiming her hold on common sense as she turned to face him.

'Just that tonight you need to sleep, and you will do so in my arms.'

'You're very sure of yourself.'

Much surer than she was that she could resist him. 'And I'm to remain in your arms until you grow tired of me and send me away?' Angling her chin, she stared up at him. 'I don't think so.'

'I've got no plans to send you away,' he said, drawing his hands down her body until the dress fell away. He steadied her as she stepped out of it, and then stepped back.

'What are you doing?' she demanded.

'I would have thought that was obvious,' he said, maintaining caution-shattering eye contact as he cupped her between her legs.

'Sleep, you said,' she accused shakily. 'And then we'll talk in the morning.'

'You will sleep. I promise,' he said.

After sex, she thought as her body overruled her caution.

'You're so deliciously plump here,' he said as he cupped and soothed and teased, applying just the right amount of pressure until she was out of her mind with lust. 'You definitely need my attention before you can sleep,' he observed in a tone she found thrillingly matter-of-fact.

So much, Millie thought as Khalid suggested in an amused whisper, 'Let's go to bed, so I can show you how much you need this.'

'And then?'

'And then you sleep,' he said dryly.

'I mean, when you go back to your life and I go back to mine.'

'That's what I'm going to talk about in the morning.'

'Put me down,' she insisted when he carried her to the bed, but it was only a token struggle. She enjoyed the banter between them, as well as everything else. It was just a pity it couldn't last, but, as he'd once said to her, he was a man and she was a woman; *carpe diem*, seize the moment, or waste more of her life regretting.

Stripping back the covers with one arm, Khalid lowered her against the nest of pillows. Maintaining eye contact, he stripped off. Damn that mix of stern and wicked. She was lost. She wanted him. Even if it was just one last time.

'I won't hurt you,' he promised.

Any more than he had already, Khalid thought.

'Sex won't hurt the baby,' she told him. 'I read up on it.'

Emotions he'd never expected to feel welled up inside him at the thought that this was the mother of his child.

'Words hurt,' she said quietly, staring deep into his eyes. 'Actions hurt. Not telling each other the truth hurts.'

He said nothing, knowing the truth could be destructive, and he would never hurt Millie.

Stretching out his length beside her, he brought her into his arms. 'I'm not joking about sleeping. I don't want to hear another word from you until the morning.'

'Like that's going to happen?' she said.

'Close your eyes,' he instructed.

'Only if you touch me.'

'Hussy,' he growled, moving over her.

'Only for you,' she whispered as she wound her arms around him.

Millie blinked and realised daylight was streaming through the curtains. 'What happened?' she asked, looking around.

'You're still wrapped in my arms and I'm in no hurry to move away,' Khalid told her in a growly, morning voice. 'I've been watching you sleep.'

'Snoring?'

He pulled a wry face. 'Not that I could hear.'

'What are you doing?' she asked. 'I'm still asleep.'

'Not for long,' he promised.

Kissing and touching, he stroked and soothed her as she whimpered and sighed. It was all too easy to fall under his spell, but when she woke up and came to her senses, what then?

'Better?' he asked as she trembled in anticipation of more pleasure to come.

'No,' she said, trying to regain a grip on reality that didn't include the mighty Sheikh of Khalifa taking up a permanent berth in King's Dock.

'How about now?'

As Khalid sank deep, she lost control immediately, which made reasoned thought impossible. Wrapping her legs tightly around him, she worked as vigorously as he did to bring them both the satisfaction they craved. After making love, they slept again, and she woke in his arms. Khalid was still sleeping—or so she thought— when she slipped out of bed to shower and dress.

'Where are you going?' he asked.

She turned to see him resting his chin on his hand as he stared at her.

'Home,' she said quietly.

There was a pause, and then he frowned and said, 'Why?'

Because this was the perfect ending, Millie thought. She'd spent so many teenage years dreaming and imagining that she knew exactly when the curtain should come down.

'There's nothing to be gained by staying any longer,' she said. 'We both know this can't go anywhere.'

'So you're leaving before we talk about the baby?'

'I'm sure you'll have your lawyers handle your side of the discussion.'

He looked astounded.

'I'll be ready for them when they arrive,' she promised calmly as her heart began to crumble like an iceberg in the sun.

'Is this because of some silly idea you have about me being a king and you being an apprentice?'

'Well, of course it has something to do with it,' she admitted. 'I'm hardly a suitable match. Don't you have an arranged bride on the horizon?'

Millie's heart shrank to the size of a pea as she waited for Khalid to reply. She could bear this, she told herself firmly. Whatever he had to say, she could take it.

'There's something I should have told you,' he said as he swung off the bed.

She prepared for the worst.

'That time…before the ball,' he began.

'When your meetings overran,' she supplied tensely. 'Were you…?' She had to brace herself to say the words. 'Were you discussing a marriage?'

'Yes, I was,' he admitted.

She swayed. He caught hold of her. 'I was discussing our marriage.'

'What?' she said faintly.

'It takes time to change the constitution of a country,' he explained as she stared up in bewilderment. 'That constitution has been changed to allow the ruler of Khalifa to choose his own bride. It's the way forward, Millie, not just for us, but for our children, and for all the future generations.'

'You did this for me,' she whispered.

'Yes, I did.'

'I don't know what to say,' Millie admitted.

'You're a self-made woman and an inspiration to everyone who meets you. And you're the mother of my child,' he added. 'The simple fact is, you're a woman and I'm a man. Do I need any more reasons?'

Perhaps one, she thought.

'And I love you,' he said.

Yes.

'I can't think of anything more important than that, can you?'

And neither could Millie. 'So…'

'So, you're not going anywhere,' Khalid said as he lifted her into his arms. 'You're staying here with me.'

'Well,' she teased, hardly able to contain her happiness, 'I suppose if I have to be anyone's captive—'

With a laugh, Khalid swung her around. 'That imagination of yours should be bottled and sold, and then I wouldn't need sapphire mines to make a fortune.'

'Another fortune?' Millie commented as her heart threatened to explode with love.

'Think of all the good you can do with my money.'

'Now, there's a suggestion I doubt anyone's heard before,' she admitted.

'Then, it's time you started thinking about it,' Khalid insisted, turning serious. 'You're the love of my life, and I want to share everything with you.'

'Are you asking me to believe that His Majesty the mighty Sheikh of Khalifa loves Millie Dillinger, oil-smeared apprentice, and sometime laundress?'

Khalid's mouth pressed down in the way she loved. 'A man called Khalid loves Millie,' he said, 'and that's the beginning and the end of it.'

'So, what are you proposing?'

Pulling back his head, he stared down at her. 'Marriage, of course.'

'Are you serious?' she gasped.

Lowering her to the ground, Khalid got down on one knee? 'Either that, or you've lost an earring. Marry me, Millie,' he said in a very different tone, 'and stand at my side for ever.'

'As your Queen?' Millie blurted, still shocked.

'As my wife,' Khalid corrected her. 'You're the only woman who is uniquely qualified for the job.'

'What qualification would that be?'

'You love me.'

'Well, yes, I do,' she admitted. 'So much it hurts.'

'Is that a yes?' Khalid demanded, his eyes burning with love and laughter. 'Can I get up now?'

'You *are* serious,' she said.

'Never more so,' he confirmed. 'I knew the moment that the young Prince hurried to escort you that I had to move heaven and earth to push that new law through. No one else could be my wife. No man could ever love you as I do. I intend to spend the rest of my life with you, and I want the whole world to know that I adore you. Starting with you,' he added softly as he cupped Millie's face in his hands.

It was a long time before they broke apart, and when they did, she remembered their talk.

'About this child or the next?' Khalid teased as he stroked her belly. 'Or all of our children to come?'

'Stop it,' she said, laughing. 'But what about my education?'

'I intend to continue that in depth.'

'I mean my college education,' she whispered against his wicked mouth.

'You can continue that at one of the best engineering colleges in the world.'

'In Khalifa,' she said.

'Exactly. If that's what you want.'

'It is what I want.'

'Good.'

'But where will we live?'

Khalid shrugged as he smiled and admitted, 'I have homes across the world. Where would you like to live?'

'In one of the transportable palaces,' Millie exclaimed softly as her imagination took her flying back to the desert.

'Maybe when the baby's a little older,' Khalid suggested. 'But we can take holidays in the meantime,' he added quickly when he saw her disappointment.

As Millie stared up into dark, beloved eyes, she knew there would never be anyone to compare with her Sapphire Sheikh, and that whatever else Khalid had to tell her about the past, they had a lifetime to understand and discuss it.

'I love you so much,' she said. 'I always have—right from that first moment when you came to my rescue like an avenging angel striding into the bowels of hell on board the *Sapphire*.'

'I never doubted it,' he said as he backed her towards the bed. 'And I love you so much, it's going to take a lifetime to prove it.'

'Starting now?' she said hopefully.

'Oh, yes,' Millie's darkly dangerous Sapphire Sheikh confirmed.

CHAPTER FIFTEEN

Millie and Khalid's arrival in Khalifa was a double celebration. Before their private jet had landed, Millie changed out of casual jeans and a lightweight top into a knee-length summer dress, garnished with a simple straw sun hat with ribbons streaming behind in the same blue as her eyes. Khalid had donned his regal royal robes of black and gold, with the crown-like *agal* holding his flowing headdress in place. They drove through streets lined with flags to herald a much-loved leader's return, in an open-topped limousine to the cheers of his people who were also celebrating the discovery of yet another rich seam of sapphires in the Khalifan mines. It was a sign, the elders had said, Khalid confided in Millie, that their leader's prospective bride would bring good fortune to their country.

'I've never been so happy,' Millie admitted. 'You love me, and that's enough,' she said as Khalid raised her hands to his lips. Which was exactly what she'd said when Khalid had placed the fabulous sapphire engagement ring on her ring finger. But he'd insisted, saying the sapphire was the same colour as her eyes. It was a huge and flawless blue, surrounded by flashing diamonds that sparkled and glowed in the blaze of the sun.

'Sapphires mean many things to many people,' Khalid had told her, when she'd said it was too much, and all she needed was him. 'To some they bring nothing but greed and grief, while to others, they foretell a lifetime of happiness ahead, and that is how it will be for you.'

She believed him, and knew that the wonderful ring was the start of their future together. The past could hold no more terrors for her. Their love had driven those shadows away.

'And now for the intimacy of the desert,' he said as the limousine turned into his private airstrip, 'where I will be joining you tomorrow.'

'The intimacy?' Millie queried, thinking of the vastness of the place she had chosen to pledge her love.

'Wherever we are, it's just the two of us,' he said.

The look in Khalid's eyes as he escorted her up the steps of the aircraft before parting from her thrilled Millie more than she could say. The prospect of being married to him still seemed incredible. 'How can I wait?' she whispered as he turned to go.

'I'll make sure you're well rewarded for your patience,' he said.

This was going to be the perfect wedding with the perfect guests and the perfect bridegroom, Millie thought,

tense with excitement as her friend Lucy helped to put
the finishing touches to Millie's flowing white lace
gown, while Miss Francine made sure the diamond
and sapphire tiara was safely secured in Millie's hair.
Khalid had only insisted on one thing in his bride, and
that was that she leave her pencil ornament behind,
and replace it with the priceless coronet for their marriage ceremony.

They were still laughing over his innovative wedding gift, which was a comprehensive tool kit, just to
let Millie know that she might be a royal bride, but she
could still be called upon to mend a boiler from time
to time. And his gifts didn't end there. There was a
snowy-white pony waiting to greet her arrival in the
desert, and when she joined her group of friends in
the bridal tent, she found them cooing over a golden
chest, studded with sapphires, which, when she opened
it, was full of the most incredible jewels, as well as
a stack of pencils. But the best thing of all was the
news that Miss Francine's laundry had been saved, and
was well on its way to becoming a highly successful franchise.

Not totally the best thing, Millie thought as she
stepped out of the tent to find Khalid waiting for her,
mounted on Bakran. 'You're not supposed to see me,'
she exclaimed.

'Too late,' he informed her. 'And as it's your wedding day, I don't know why you're hesitating.'

'I'm not,' she said, seizing hold of his hand.

In seconds she was on the back of his fiery stallion,

and, to cheers from her friends, they galloped across the desert to the shore of the oasis where the crowd of guests were waiting to welcome the Sheikh of Khalifa and his Queen.

EPILOGUE

*Eight years, one engineering qualification,
four children, and a newborn baby later...*

'A PENCIL IN your hair?' Khalid demanded as their old-
est child, Luna, a gorgeous, bubbly tomboy, consulted
her clipboard and frowned.

'The entire palace air-con needs a complete refurb,'
Luna informed her father in a tone that exactly mim-
icked her mother's.

'And I know the very person to supervise these
works,' Khalid said as he drew Millie close.

'I'm quite capable of supervising my own works,'
Luna assured him.

'By pressing your brothers and sisters into work?'
Khalid suggested fondly. 'Come on, time for bed.'

Millie helped him chivvy the children out of the
family snug they had created in their magnificent palace in Khalifa. 'It's adult time now,' he added with a
glance in Millie's direction.

Would she never get enough of this man? Millie
wondered as she took in Khalid's magnificent phy-

sique, shown off to best advantage in snug-fitting jeans and a close-fitting top. He'd had taught her everything about love and trust, and feeling safe—as well as the most incredible sex.

'It's a very important part of marriage,' he told her when they had finished the bedtime stories and closed the door on their sleeping children.

'I would never disagree,' she said.

'Yes, you would,' Khalid argued dryly. Drawing her into his nearby study, he closed the door.

'I would never argue about this,' she whispered as he kissed her neck and backed her up against the wall. Dispensing with the clothes that stood in his way, he lifted her. 'But can I remind you that we're hosting a royal banquet in less than an hour.'

'Then, you'll have to be quick,' he said.

'With you?'

He shrugged. 'I'll make up for it,' he promised. 'Just concentrate and let me do the work.'

Okay, he was right. He hadn't even touched her yet, and she was already hovering on the brink. 'You've made me mad for you,' she said.

'Are you pregnant again?' he queried. 'That always makes you mad for sex.'

'*You* make me mad for sex,' she corrected him.

'That too,' he agreed.

'Modesty would become you.'

'But it wouldn't satisfy you.' And with that, he proceeded to tease her into an advance state of readiness. 'So. Are you pregnant?' he asked when she was quiet again.

'We can only hope,' Millie whispered.

'And trust,' Khalid added, 'but as we don't have much time, and I feel the need again, we'll talk about this later.'

'Yes, Your Majesty,' Millie said, sharing his smile.

'This is the only time I can ever get you to obey,' Khalid complained as he positioned her for pleasure.

'Be grateful for small mercies.'

'Small?'

'Okay, not small,' she gasped as he took her in one firm thrust. And now it was impossible to speak at all.

She would never tire of this man and the family they were building. This was her life, her love, her every-thing. 'You're a very bad man,' she scolded as Khalid began to move with real intent.

'Yes, I am,' he agreed. 'Thank goodness I found such a bad woman to match me.'

* * * * *

#3637 HIS MILLION-DOLLAR MARRIAGE PROPOSAL

The Powerful Di Fiore Tycoons

by Jennifer Hayward

Lazzero needs a fake fiancée to win a business deal. He offers to absolve Chiara's father's bankruptcy, *if* she wears his ring! But with their explosive attraction, soon Lazzero wants Chiara as his—for good!

#3638 TYCOON'S FORBIDDEN CINDERELLA

by Melanie Milburne

Lucien refuses to indulge in love, but delectable Audrey tests his control! Her shy innocence holds an enticing appeal. When scandal forces them together, Lucien proposes a temporary solution to their cravings—delicious surrender!

#3639 BOUND TO HER DESERT CAPTOR

Conveniently Wed!

by Michelle Conder

Certain that Regan has information on his sister's disappearance, Sheikh Jaeger steals her away to his palace. But when beautiful, defiant Regan accidentally causes a media storm, to resolve it Jaeger *must* marry her!

#3640 A MISTRESS, A SCANDAL, A RING

Ruthless Billionaire Brothers

by Angela Bissell

For Xavier, seducing stunning Jordan is a calculated risk. He's convinced their fire will soon burn out. But when their affair's exposed, there's just one option—bind Jordan to him permanently!

Get 4 FREE REWARDS!

We'll send you 2 FREE Books
<u>plus</u> 2 FREE Mystery Gifts.

Harlequin Presents® books feature a sensational and sophisticated world of international romance where sinfully tempting heroes ignite passion.

FREE Value Over **$20**

"I can see you are not asleep" came a familiar voice from much
too close. "It is best to stop pretending, Sophie."

It was a voice that should not have been anywhere near her,
not here.

Not in Langston House where, in a few short hours, she would
become the latest in a long line of unenthused countesses.

Sophie took her time turning over in her bed. And still, no
matter how long she stared or blinked, she couldn't make Renzo
disappear.

"What are you doing here?" she asked, her voice barely more
than a whisper.

"It turns out we have more to discuss."

She didn't like the way he said that, dark and something like
lethal.

And Renzo was here.

Right here, in this bedroom Sophie had been installed in as the
future Countess of Langston. It was all tapestries, priceless art and
frothy antique chairs that looked too fragile to sit in.

"I don't know what you mean," she said, her lips too dry and
her throat not much better.

"I think you do." Renzo stood at the foot of her bed, one hand looped around one of the posts in a lazy, easy sort of grip that did absolutely nothing to calm Sophie's nerves. "I think you came to tell me something last night but let my temper scare you off. Or perhaps it would be more accurate to say you used my temper as an excuse to keep from telling me, would it not?"

Sophie found her hands covering her belly again, there beneath her comforter. Worse, Renzo's dark gaze followed the movement, as if he could see straight through the pile of soft linen to the truth.

"I would like you to leave," she told him, fighting to keep her voice calm. "I don't know what showing up here, hours before I'm meant to marry, could possibly accomplish. Or is this a punishment?"

Renzo's lips quirked into something no sane person would call a smile. He didn't move and yet he seemed to loom there, growing larger by the second and consuming all the air in the bedchamber.

He made it hard to breathe. Or see straight.

"We will get to punishments in a moment," Renzo said. His dark amber gaze raked over her, bold and harsh. His sensual mouth, the one she'd felt on every inch of her skin and woke in the night yearning for again, flattened. His gaze bored into her, so hard and deep she was sure he left marks. "Are you with child, Sophie?"

Don't miss
THE BRIDE'S BABY OF SHAME,
available July 2018.

*And the first part of the **STOLEN BRIDES** duet,*
KIDNAPPED FOR HIS ROYAL DUTY by Jane Porter.

Available now
wherever Harlequin Presents® books and ebooks are sold.

www.Harlequin.com